Under
the
Red Umbrella

VALE ROYAL WRITERS GROUP

ACKNOWLEDGEMENTS

Cover design by JT Lindroos
Cover photograph by Aaron Amat
Edited by Tonia Bevins, Lee Howell,
Liz Sandbach and Debbie Bennett

Special thanks to *The Blue Cap* in Sandiway for hosting our
meetings and providing refreshments.

INTRODUCTION

A collection of short stories, prose and poetry to celebrate ten years of the **Vale Royal Writers Group** in Cheshire.

Members come from all walks of life – some no longer live in Cheshire but remain associated with the group, joined by their love of our county and of writing.

VRWG meet monthly in Sandiway. For more information, check out **www.vrwg.co.uk** or find us on facebook at **www.facebook.com/groups/ValeRoyalWritersGroup/**

CONTENTS

Tonia Bevins

NORTHWICH UNDER THE SKIN

I am your taxi driver peddling knock-off cigarettes,
the pensioner beside you in the pet shop
after a harness and lead for the ferret.
I am the old biker lady, all studs and chains,
crumpled white face above a black leather vest.
I am the hamster brought out unhurt from the blazing flat,
supplying your all-time favourite headline.
I am the tattooed man, every visible inch of skin inked out in
green:
I forgive your gobsmacked stare each time you see me.
I am the man with the withered arm sweeping litter in the park,
the ones 'going Tesco', 'going Bingo'
because who wastes a preposition these word-strapped times?
I am the drama queen on the midnight skyline,
the stage-set chemical plant fizzing in the limelight.

I am the fast-food joints and 'We Buy Gold',
the nail bars, pound stores and boarded up pubs.
I am the underbelly, the unprovoked attack,
five against one outside the chip shop
on a street that's dead by 9.00pm.
I am the old merchants' subdivided villas,
the new all-day-lonely dollhouse estates.
I am sixties civic concrete and jacked-up black-and-whites,
blue bridges, meanders and graceful flights of locks.
I am long, secret lanes leading nowhere.

I am coarse and salty, I give you that sinking/rising feeling,
your sliced white going round all night:
you breathe in the aroma as you skim the bypass,
finding yourself ravenous for toast.

I am the reek of drains invading your nostrils
where streets run down to the river.
I am tight enough you're on nodding terms with strangers.
I have edged out far enough into a hinterland
of hamlets and business parks to retain my mystery.
I am every northern town yet like no other.
I am the one you know in your bones like a long-lost sister,
the one you sometimes don't know at all,
the one you defend but haven't earned the right to mock,
the one you'd weep for if you could ever leave.

PUDDLES

Mark Acton

Nigel liked the rain when he was driving his new car, mostly because the wipers actually worked on this one and *actually* wiped the beating rain from his windscreen, allowing him to see what was actually outside on the road in front of him, rather than just smearing dirty wet blobs across his face, the way that his old car did. Mostly, what was in front of him were people in other, inferior cars craning their necks and straining their eyes to see what impending doom might befall them from the other side of their Jackson Pollock-style smudged windscreens; or pedestrians struggling against the wind with feeble umbrellas whose frames battle like newborn Bambi legs against the elements.

But in this car, Nigel was king, and he knew that everyone who saw him drive by simultaneously wanted to be him and hated him, and that fuelled his favourite thing about the rain: pissing off pedestrians – or 'peasant baiting', as he liked to call it. And the best targets were those poor unfortunates who had to catch the bus. Not only did they suffer the indignity of sharing a dilapidated slaughter truck with hundreds of other disease-ridden, bath-avoiding livestock, but they also had to pay for the privilege of sitting, or standing, in a vehicle that was not capable of going more than 200 yards without stopping; and having their ears assaulted by the laboured chugging of the diesel engine, the tinny rattle of mp3 players, and the semi-intelligible ramblings of teenage girls on their mobile phones, who had degraded their written English to a poor phonetic representation of the way that they spoke and then degraded their speech to an inarticulate representation of the way that they texted.

But worse than any of that, these poor vermin were forced to wait outside in queues in the cold and pouring rain for the honour of this experience. If that wasn't enough, the Minister for Shitty Transport had decreed that all bus stops must be built at the side of the road next to where the largest puddles are likely to form, in order to present the biggest possible stationary target for people like Nigel to hit. Nigel loved that Minister; he wanted to be that Minister one day, and today Nigel was going to take full advantage of the great gift that the Minister had offered.

So, there it was. One huge puddle on the side of the road and one open bus stop with a chain gang of victims resignedly awaiting their fate and not sure which they were dreading more: the soaking, or the bus journey.

The beauty for Nigel with this puddle was that the pedestrians were a couple of feet back so he would have to pick up a bit of pace to make sure the spray got high enough to do some proper damage. *You want to get the face: the eyes and the mouth; any of the sensory organs.* He revved the engine and put his foot down.

The water sounded like a cymbal crash as he hit it and it cascaded into the air in slow motion towards its flinching target, as if it were a 1980s power ballad pop video. Nigel cocked his head back and laughed, staring out of his passenger window.

And then he sank like a stone.

As the drenched commuters started to regain their composure, if not their dignity, they stared back at the road and the puddle and saw no signs of Nigel or his car, except for a few bubbles on the surface.

"That'll teach him to go after my job," said the Minister for Shitty Transport, watching the CCTV footage from behind his desk. "Little shit," he said, and stubbed out his cigar.

Stephanie Acton

I WANT TO LIVE A BIT BEFORE I DIE

I want to live a bit before I die
Don't want to be left waiting
I want to live between the words I write

I want to go but still I lag behind
Just watching, not partaking
I want to live a bit before I die

I want to shed in layers where I lie
Too tired, procrastinating
I want to live between the words I write

I want to feel like now it is my time
Sit ready for the making
I want to live a bit before I die

I want to turn the darkness into light
Pour out, and never faking
I want to live between the words I write

I want to grasp this power in my sight
And take it, not forsaking
I want to live a bit before I die
To live between the words I want to write

Liz Sandbach

THE FUSTIAN CUTTERS

The fustian masters of Manchester
sent out their rolls of cloth
to the northern towns and villages
where labour costs were leaner.

In Dierden Street the women worked
twelve hours at a shift
as up and down the length of cloth
they cut the cotton wefts.

To cut a piece of cloth
of 75 yards length
they'd walk 36 long miles
back and to along the bench.

To produce good-quality fustian
meant 40 cuts per inch
and they paid for any mistakes
so really felt the pinch.

With pounding head and aching back
they laboured in the heat,
in the dusty, lint-filled air
till their lungs were clogged and weak.

Mothers toiled from morn till night
for very little pay
and a child was often brought to them
to suckle thrice a day.

Or they brought their babies with them,
quiet from opium-taking,
that wrapped them in the sleep
that sometimes knew no waking.

Babies thin and listless,
pitiable, wizened, small,
grew up frail, stunted, brain damaged.
Or didn't grow up at all.

So from those fustian factories
some gained but others lost,
for as so often happened,
it came at a human cost.

COMING HOME

Joan Dowling

The shock was coming in waves now and Mel's compulsive circuits around the hospital room gathered speed, as if she could outpace the fear that threatened to overwhelm her. She was shaking uncontrollably and felt that the frantic pacing was all that stopped her legs from giving way completely. On the bed, Dee remained frighteningly still, her face dirty and drained, her grubby hands an insult on the crisp, white sheet that covered her. Tubes and cables coiled in every direction and a screen glowed greenly in the dim light of the ICU. Apart from Mel's rhythmic footsteps, only occasional warning bleeps from the machines broke the church-like silence.

"Are you alright?" Mel was startled when the nurse pushed open the door. "Here, drink this. You're in shock and it will help." The nurse managed to sound both disapproving and solicitous at the same time. Placing a cup and saucer on the table, she gestured to the chair beside it and Mel sat, heavily. She lifted the cup with trembling hands and sipped the scalding tea. The nurse was right. After a few minutes, the combination of hot tea and sugar started to calm her and her breathing steadied. She leaned back in the chair and tried to relax. The nurse was busy at Dee's side.

"What's her name? D'you know what she's taken – or how we can reach her family?" Gently stroking Dee's forehead, the nurse continued almost inaudibly. "There's a mother out there somewhere – waiting."

"I only know she's called Dee. I don't know her. I just met her tonight, down by the river, near the weir." Mel's lie was automatic, as all her lies were now. "She was sitting on a bench and we got talking. Then she started to sound funny and just fell on the ground. I used my mobile to call the ambulance and when it came, they asked me to come here with her." She stared resentfully at the nurse. "I didn't have to do that, you know."

The nurse looked sceptical, then her face softened. "You did the right thing. But it might already be too late. Whatever she took, it could have been some time before you met her and the damage had probably been done by then."

"You mean she could die?" Mel tried to keep the panic out of her voice.

"I honestly don't know, it depends if we got to her in time. But there could be others. That stretch of the riverbank is a Mecca for the local druggies. If she's shared something that's been contaminated, she probably won't be the only one we see here tonight. Anyway, the police are on their way – they'll take care of it all. They'll probably want to ask you some questions, too." Smiling now, she added, "Do you want some more tea?"

Mel jumped to her feet. "No. I want to use the toilet; where is it?"

"Through the double doors, second on the left. But don't be too long. The police could be here any minute."

Mel left the room, shielding her eyes against the sudden harsh brightness in the corridor. She found the Ladies and went straight to the sink, filled the bowl with cold water and lifted handfuls to her face. Drying herself on a paper towel, she slumped against the wall and breathed deeply for several minutes. She needed time to think – but not here. Outside in the corridor again, she put her head down and moved quickly, following the Way Out signs until she reached the exit. At the front door, she hesitated, undecided; then she started to run.

When she reached the squat, Mel wasn't surprised to find that there was no one there. They'd all been at the river together tonight, as they were most nights. Although Mel found the heavy drug scene scary, she usually went with them because she didn't know what else to do. Tonight there'd been talk of meeting a new supplier and the gang were on a high before they even left the house. Mel had barely registered the stranger briefly in amongst them at the river, but she had noticed the numbers dwindle as people started to drift away.

Dee was one of the few who hung around and Mel stayed with her. Then, suddenly, Dee grasped her arm, took a long, shuddering breath and collapsed at her feet. The rest of the group scattered rapidly – Jed calling out to Mel that she should get away. Fast. She'd started to do as he said, then she'd stopped – turned back. While none of the group could really be called friends, she and Dee had a sort of understanding. When Mel had arrived in the city two weeks earlier, she'd spent a couple of terrifying nights in a shop doorway. On the third day, she'd met Dee at the soup kitchen and Dee offered to take her back to the squat.

"It's not much, but it's better than sleeping on the street," she'd said.

Dee had been high when they met and she and Mel had talked for hours, compared depressingly similar stories – the chaotic schools, truancy, dropping out, then the helpless slide into drink and drugs. Confused and disappointed parents had resorted to increasingly desperate punishments that had finally driven both girls out onto the streets. As night fell, Dee became tearful and dragged a tattered envelope out of a box under her bed. "My family," she'd said, showing creased photographs of parents, brothers and a sister. And she'd wept as she stuffed them back into the envelope.

Mel was grateful for the squat but she was unnerved by the frightening amount of drink and drugs around. Before she fled from home, her father had yelled that no drugs were recreational, that they all led to the gutter and she was already halfway there. He should see this lot, Mel had thought dismally when she arrived at the squat. The place demoralised her. Cold and squalid, all it offered was shelter. Although friendly, its occupants were unpredictable and distant and she soon realised that their days were spent planning how to get hold of enough alcohol and drugs to sustain them through the night. Within a week, Mel had seen enough to make her long to return home but the memory of her mother's troubled face and her father's deep disappointment had paralysed her.

Now, she realised, she would have to make a move. The

police knew about this place and they would come here soon. Gathering up her few clothes, she stuffed them into a plastic carrier bag and left by the back door, heading for the main road. Several times she stopped and had to resist the temptation to go back. If only she'd thought to look in Dee's box, there might have been an address – maybe she could have called Dee's family, warned them before the police got to them. Prepared them for the shock that was coming their way.

The nurse's voice echoed in her head – *a mother somewhere, waiting*. Pulling out her mobile phone, Mel found the familiar number and punched the keys. Her text was brief. "Mum, I'm coming home."

Alex Bell

MOVING

Another box emptied, another
box ticked. Another move
to find myself lost amongst
corrugated containers,
containing remains
of this life, my life. A life filled
with prevarication, medication,
intoxication. Intoxicated
feelings as scrunched up
as last week's newspapers:
newspapers, filling the void,
avoiding breakages, feeling
less bold than headlines
that clamber off pages
down through gaps
between floorboards.
Floored frame of somewhere
I've never been, seduced
by baited picture hooks.
Constellations upon night
sky wall, 100 watt
full moon sending nothing
crazy but a moth, stealing light
one wing beat at a time.
Containers crash open,
leaving love's debris
on display. Traverse
loft ladders to discreet
old love letters, words
for the eyes of a young
man, buried amongst

the rubble of a life left
behind, boxed up
and stored
for safekeeping,
protected from
the bitter heart
of this old man.
Protecting this
bitter man
from his
heart.

THE WINTER CRUISE

Joyce Ireland

From the bow, using the two-way radio, Roger called to Carol: "Boat approaching, love. He's closer to the bridge."

Carol reduced the revs and briefly put the engine into reverse. She couldn't see clearly as the low winter sun dazzled her twice, once directly and then from its reflection in the canal. The narrowboat slowed to a stop and they waited.

"How are we doing?" she called to Roger.

"Hang on. He doesn't seem to be making much headway. He is quite close to the bridge though."

Minutes passed. Carol steadied the boat using the forward and reverse gears.

"Think he's about to come through. When we clear this bridge I'll put the kettle on and ..." He broke off suddenly.

Carol called back. "What's that? I've lost you."

Still silence.

"Roger?"

"Carol – he's gone!"

"What do you mean? Is he coming through yet?"

"No ... he's disappeared. I don't understand – he was there one minute then ... Carol, can you get us through and we'll moor up. I need to think."

A few minutes later, the boat secured, Carol looked at her husband. He seemed quite upset. "What happened? Are you all right? Was there a boat or not. I can't see one in either direction."

They gazed up and down the cut; no boats or people in sight anywhere.

"Sure you didn't dream it?" Carol tried to make light of it.

"No. I'm sure it was there. I remember thinking the guy steering looked a bit strange and the boat was a traditional boat, with a tarp instead of a cabin, maybe a kids' camping boat. Oh, I don't know. I just feel a bit of a fool now."

"Let's make a cuppa, then we can carry on. Let's get to the Royal Oak and tie up there. It's only a few minutes away."

With the boat securely moored they sat in the front cabin drinking tea, Roger still looking thoughtful, Carol trying not to worry about it. After all, there must be a reasonable explanation.

Suddenly, Roger looked up. "That sounds like a Bolinder engine. I always wanted a boat with one of those but I know I don't have the mechanical know-how to look after one properly. Sounds good though."

He went to the window to see what kind of boat was about to pass. As he waited he visualised the engine, doubtless all its brasses lovingly polished, the oil dispenser and the large fly wheel which combined to make the deep rhythmic thump as it turned the propeller.

The sound swelled and was soon very close. Then it began to fade. The water of the canal remained calm and undisturbed as it had been. No boat had appeared and there was no sign of a wash.

"Now what? Was it a trad boat?"

"I don't know. I didn't see anything." Roger sat down and picked up his mug of tea. "I think I'm going mad." He was quite pale.

Carol said, "No, love, you're not mad. I heard the sound too. There must be an explanation but I don't know what. Let's tie up nearer the pub. Maybe someone else saw or heard something."

Sitting with a couple of pints of best bitter they mulled over the events of the afternoon. In the warmth and brightness of the bar, surrounded by normal people beginning their weekend, things seemed much better and they began to relax.

They chatted to the young couple at the next table, who introduced themselves as Mick and Alison James, from the boat astern of theirs.

"Seen many other boats out today?' Roger asked casually.

"Only a couple of small cruisers, heading up to Chester, an

hour or so before lunch. That was it, wasn't it, Mick?" Alison glanced at her husband.

"Mmm, yes, I think so. Mind I did think I saw a very old wooden narrowboat coming towards us at one point. But when I went up on deck there was nothing in sight." He grinned. "Must have been that pint I had at lunchtime."

Carol urged him on. "Where was it; near bridge 108 above Wharton Lock? What did it sound like?"

Mick thought for a minute. "Yes. It had a thumping noise, different from ours certainly."

"You mean a Bolinder; you know the old single-cylinder, low-revving engine that the old workboats used?"

"If you say so, mate. I wouldn't know."

They all finished their meals, had a couple more drinks and wished each other good night.

At about four in the morning, Roger awoke with a start, not sure at first what had disturbed him. Then he heard the *thump, thump* of that engine again. Carol lay beside him, also awake. "Shall we go and look?" she said.

They put on fleeces and waterproofs against the cold. Opening the hatch nervously, Roger looked around. There was nothing in sight. The full moon lit up the canal tow path and with the stars it was possible to make out the shapes of trees, the other boat and the pub; but nothing moved.

Suddenly, there was a bright flash and a low-pitched thud. Momentarily blinded, they clung to each other.

"What was that? No one else seems to have noticed." Carol felt on the verge of hysteria.

"I don't know. Let's get in out of the cold. I'll put the kettle on."

They sat and drank coffee till daylight, then Roger went out to look at the place the flash had appeared to be. There was nothing untoward to be seen. An old man walking along the tow path stopped beside Roger, gazing into the water.

"You looking for Joe Cawston? This was where him and his boat were blown up and they do say it can still be seen about this time of year."

"Who d'you mean? Who sees him?" Roger turned to him.

"During the war, about 1943, this fellow was taking some explosive stuff to the munitions factory near Chester. He hit a bridge and bang! That was the last of him. Sometimes it's folks on the boats, sometimes it's folks walking along as see him; but it's always in this second week in December."

Roger and Carol decided that they'd had enough mystery for one winter. They packed up and went home!

Tonia Bevins

LIVERPOOL GHAZAL

What is this bay, this river mouth, this port, this Liverpool,
Spring Anchorage lipped on the green pool of Liverpool?

On the Atlantic suck and spit of tides, the gathered in
and the outcast drift; the past, so casually cruel to Liverpool.

The Garston bus, early doors in empty bars still bring you
back.
I was your plaything for a while, your fool in Liverpool.

On Hardman Street Somali women smile and traffic slows;
in rainbow jalabeeb they glow like jewels in Liverpool.

These sledgehammer hot nights music spills through open
windows:
salsa, dancehall, Elgar, rock 'n' roll – so cool in Liverpool.

Billy Fury, teen idol, I wish you'd stayed in Dingle.
London unlaced your soundtrack from the spool, its Liverpool.

Banana box tarantulas scuttle from the docks by night:
urban myth or truth? Send Java plums, sweet jambul to
Liverpool.

City of dreamers, where fortunes wax and wane like the moon.
Keep one eye on the horizon is the rule in Liverpool.

Your stowaway poet, incomer, incast, fears exile
with sea monsters in Ultima Thule – ah, Liverpool.

Liverpool Ghazal *was commended in the 2013 Bedford Open Poetry Competition and
first published in* The Interpreter's House.

EXTRA TIME

Marian Smith

Norm is transfixed, but he can hear a persistent voice just behind his left ear.

"Tea?"

"No."

"No what?"

"No and for God's sake shut up."

"Very polite, I don't think."

Gary Lineker is commentating. He is getting very excited. "... And it's Argentina 2, England 1 with only three minutes to go until the end of extra time."

"Sandwich?"

"No ... yes ... later ..."

"Beef or ham?"

"Don't care."

"Make your bloody mind up."

"Beef."

"With pickle or tomato?"

"Whatever."

The smell of hair spray and rancid chip oil recedes. Doris is shuffling back to the kitchen muttering, her carpet slippers slapping against the calloused soles of her bare feet. Then, she stops and turns and her voice comes through again, as if she has some internal volume control that she is slowly turning up to maximum. "Your mother rang this morning."

Norm is ignoring her.

"I said ... your mother rang this morning."

Norm is gripping the edge of the sofa. His bald head is shining with greasy sweat. He is trying to pretend she isn't there.

It is now in the last minute of extra time. There is uproar. Steven Gerrard has broken away and is tearing down the left wing. Unmarked, he is only yards from the goal mouth. He strikes, and the ball flies past the goalkeeper's outstretched arms and into the back of the net.

Norm is on his feet. He is screaming. He is screaming so loud that he doesn't hear Doris crashing to the floor in the kitchen. But then, as the commotion on the TV subsides and he sits down again, waiting for the penalty shoot-out which could take England into the final of the World Cup, he hears a strange noise.

Doris is lying on the floor, eyes staring, mouth wide open. Norm whispers to himself: "Oh shit."

He grabs the phone from the sideboard. Presses 9 once, twice.

Norm is standing at the kitchen door, still holding the phone. He stares at Doris, then at the TV, then back at Doris again. She must have slid down the side of the kitchen unit because her wool plaid skirt is now gathered around her hips exposing her bare legs. He can't remember the last time he saw Doris's thighs. His eyes are drawn towards the smooth waxen skin and then down to her calves, veined like Stilton cheese. It is then that he notices that she is still holding the china plate but the beef sandwich has fallen to the floor.

Now he hears Gary Lineker behind him. "... And Wayne Rooney is going to take the first penalty."

There is still time.

Norm puts down the phone, and walks towards Doris. He bends down slowly.

He picks up the sandwich and opens it like a book.

Branston Pickle. His favourite.

WHEREWITHAL

Bill Webster

"'Wherewithal'. That's a good word," she said, looking up from her book. "It's a word you can really get your mouth around, don't you think?"

He grunted from behind his paper.

"'Wherewithal' *sounds* like what it *means*. It *has* substance, and it *means* substance."

"Does it, pumpkin?"

"Well of course it does, Ronald. Everyone knows that."

"Check it in the dictionary, dear. You might get a surprise. Chambers is over there on the bottom shelf." He pointed to the book without lifting his eyes from the paper.

"You are an old Luddite!" She put her book down and turned to the laptop on the coffee table. "I can do it on here. I just go to Google ..."

He sighed in exasperation and shook his head.

"... and I type in 'define wherewithal', and voilà!" She looked at him triumphantly and then read from the screen. "'Wherewithal'; noun; the necessary means, especially financial means; for example: didn't have the *wherewithal* to survive an economic downturn."

He put his *Telegraph* crossword down and padded over to the bookshelf, frowning at her through his bifocals. "How many times do I have to tell you that the internet is populated by pimply adolescents who don't know their 'wherewithal' from their 'how's your father'? Let's see what *Chambers Twentieth Century* has to say about it."

"But Ronald, this is the twenty *first* century now." She smiled. "Just when was that threadbare old thing published anyway?"

He squinted at the volume then looked her in the eye. "1961."

She laughed. "1961 … the year I started secondary school! That book is almost as old as us for goodness sake! I must get you a new one for Christmas, or better still get you on a computer course at college."

"Patricia Adamson, Hell will freeze over before you'll get me using one of these soul-sapping instruments of the devil! Now, prepare yourself for the *correct* definition of 'wherewithal'." He flicked pages back and forth as he hunted for the word.

"Your lips are moving, Ronald."

"Rubbish. Only old people move their lips when they're reading. Ah! Here we are. It's a noun." He looked up at her. "Well at least they got that bit right. It says here it means 'the means'."

"It means 'the means'? What do you mean, it means 'the means'?"

"Well what on earth do you think I mean? I mean that the meaning of your word is 'the means'."

"But what does that *mean*, Ronald? I understood my definition that I got on Google but I don't think I understand yours." She looked at him. "I don't think you understand it either, do you?"

"There's no need to be silly about this, Patricia. I know you're just trying to prove that your infernal machine is better than my books. Well it just won't do. I still have to finish the crossword before I go to meet James at The Bull."

She folded her arms and stared somewhere over his left shoulder.

"Oh! Now you're in one of your womanly moods. It's just not good enough. I really must get ready for my meeting with James. Can't this wait until later?"

She said nothing, just smiled and started tapping her foot theatrically.

He sighed. "Oh! Alright then! Let's take a quick look at Webster's. I'm sure we picked a copy up at the Scout jumble sale last year." He rummaged amongst the mess of books on the shelves.

"Webster's *is* available online nowadays you know."

Ronald feigned deafness, and then gave a little grunt of satisfaction as he retrieved a thick blue and red paperback from the top shelf. "Ha! 2002, this one, dear! Is that *twenty first century* enough for you? Now let me find your bloody silly word and we'll soon put an end to this nonsense."

"Your lips are …"

He held a finger up in admonition, and looked down sternly. "Hmm … Well that's very strange. It doesn't seem to be here. This isn't much of a dictionary, I must say."

"It must be there, darling. It's hardly an unusual word."

He walked over and knelt down, their two greying heads consulting the text together.

"See. 'Wheedle', then 'wheel', then straight to 'whet' and 'whiff'! Not a 'wher'-anything, anywhere in sight. It must be American or something. Bloody boy scouts! I've got a good mind to ask for my money back."

She wrinkled her nose in puzzlement and then laughed gently and kissed him on the cheek. "Oh, Ronnie…"

She took his hand in hers and turned it over so that the cover of the book was uppermost. Taking his index finger in her other hand, she used it to slowly underline the title 'Dictionary and Thesaurus'.

He raised his eyebrows and smiled self-deprecatingly, then leafed back to the dictionary section.

"Your lips are moving, Ronnie."

Her finger traced the outline of his lips and the book fell unnoticed to the floor.

"Ronnie?"

"Yes, pumpkin?"

He gently stroked her high cheekbones with the tips of his fingers.

"Maybe we need to work through an example to properly understand this most annoying word."

"What sort of an example did you have in mind, old girl?"

She leaned forward and kissed him softly on the lips, then smiled into his eyes. "Are you beginning to get the idea, *old* man?"

He smiled back as he folded her gently into his arms. "Mmm ... I do think I am beginning to catch on."

"So, Mr Adamson, if we were to go back upstairs for just a little while, do you think an *old* man might just possibly manage..."

She left the words hanging as they rose together and he led her towards the hall.

"Yes, Mrs Adamson, I do believe that we have the wherewithal!"

"Mmmm ... Now that's a definition I can understand! Oh! What about James and your important meeting?"

"Bugger James! Let him find his own wherewithal!"

Their footsteps receded up the stairs as the laptop whispered softly in the empty room.

Nick Monks

CRETE LULLABY

So I decided to stay and taste wine –
to dine and walk and breathe more, and sit
watching the way shadows play on white stucco houses;
to hear again, and for the first time the sea-harps and violins,
the Cretan rockrose, the mandrake, Jerusalem sage –
the sun wandering across the sky. To leave then come back.

Operation Mercury: 30,000 died on both sides. Use of
paratroopers.

All day and night Plato builds an acropolis –
pondering maps of Mediterranean islands –
Socrates soothed by waves asks questions.

Salt and honey paint my kidneys, liver, pancreas, bone, tissue,
eyes, soul:
red, blue, green like mountain flower petals,
the way a glass of wine takes 2,500 years
to capture the elements it mirrors –
the elements working on the vines, the cellar barrels.

Then I decided to leave, go to Athens and then the north.

I can still taste the dark passionate women in doorways,
the flower petals, the secret coves, the way her black hair fell
down.

Liz Wells

SPLINTERED GLASS

Emotions run so deep and dark
unnoticed by others, harsh and stark.
Insides breaking with such force
like splintered glass, no remorse.
When will the pain subside and go? Not today, it surges so
with strength that seems to gain might.
Ferocious vigour, no ease in sight.
Hard to take a breath to calm and keep the mind away from harm.
The tears that stream and sting the skin
that's saturated deep to the brim.
No relief, no let up.
On it goes, overflowing cup.
Reckless sleep, nightmares come, the split second of normal,
on waking, it's all undone.
Reality hits – another day – should feel easier, so they say.
Days get harder the more time goes on.
Losing any sense of worth through teary, swollen eyes.
How to erase the immense pain
in isolation while others continue to feign
some sort of sympathy to ease their guilt
that a human heart is broken and pain-filled to the hilt?

MOIRA

Debbie Bennett

"Are you an angel?"

"Excuse me?" I glance around the shop. An elderly couple stand by the prescriptions counter and a pregnant girl in a tartan mini-skirt – barely more than a child herself – is checking out the cold remedies. We're not exactly busy, considering it's early January and the sales shoppers are out and about on the High Street, looking for bargains.

"Are you an angel?" the voice asks again, this time accompanied by a gentle tug on my sleeve. Looking down, I see a small girl staring up at me with an expression of utter joy.

"Hello, sweetheart." I put down the box of special-offer shampoos. "What makes you think that, honey?"

"You look like a pretty angel. But my mummy says angels are only in heaven."

My own mother has certainly never compared me to an angel. In fact she frequently tells me that long blonde hair is unbecoming on somebody of my age and situation. She just can't bring herself to say the word *divorced*, as if it might somehow be catching. She still calls Ian her son-in-law – in fact, she still calls Ian more often than she calls me.

I crouch down so that I am at eye level. She's a pretty little thing, dressed in cheap denim leggings and supermarket trainers, her hair in two bunches. She has pierced ears adorned with plastic ladybird studs.

"Where's your mummy, sweetheart?"

"Buying something to make her better." She points to the pregnant girl – *teenager* – across the shop. That figures. She must have been all of fifteen when she had this one and already well on the way to the next.

"And what's your name?"

"Moira Martin. I'm three," she says proudly, then claps a

hand over her mouth. There are sudden tears at the corners of her eyes. "Mummy says I mustn't tell my name to strangers."

Moira. The name catches in my mouth, dry and sharp. For a moment I am transported back four years and I am holding my own Moira in my arms. She's wearing a sleepsuit with tiny pink rabbits on it and she's five weeks premature and so light: only three pounds and ten ounces. Three pounds, ten ounces and stillborn.

"But I'm not a stranger," I say carefully. "I work right here in this shop." Her mother isn't paying any attention to us and if I wasn't here, little Moira would probably be out in the street by now, underneath a bus. Mummy wouldn't be shopping then, would she?

"What's *your* name?" Moira asks directly.

"It says my name right here," I say, pointing to my name badge. "Angela. Your mummy should—"

"So you *are* an angel!" She jumps up and down. "I knew you were!"

Her mother looks up at the outburst, smiles slightly and takes the box she is holding to the till. I wonder what kind of parent lets her child out of sight – one with a *nose-stud* perhaps? She has a lip-ring too.

My Moira would be older than this girl. She'd have bunches too, tied high with pink ribbons. Ian and I would take her to the park, to the swings on a Sunday afternoon, before feeding the ducks and then home for a roast dinner. Ian and I would still be together and we'd be a real family. But I couldn't forgive myself for whatever my body had done or not done, and I don't think Ian could either. Irreconcilable differences, the divorce papers said, but really they could just as easily have said one word. *Moira.*

And I wonder whether this might be my Moira. Am I being given another chance to be the mother I was meant to be? I have money; my share of the house has been earning interest these past years, waiting for an opportunity for me to start my life again. I have a passport and I have my Moira's birth certificate. My purse and keys are in my pocket.

"Can you keep a secret?" I whisper. We are still alone and the door is so close.

She nods, eyes wide. "My mummy says you should never tell a secret."

"This one is special, because you must be very special to have seen that I'm an angel. Nobody else knows."

Her mouth opens to speak, but she just reaches out and touches my hair. Her hands and coat are grubby and stained with chocolate, but I don't mind. I will buy her new clothes, new toys and a new life. We will be happy, Moira and me.

"Would you like to see the other angels?" I stand up slowly, taking her hand and edging towards the shop door.

"Will my daddy be there?"

"We'll talk to daddy later," I promise. But as we get to the door, there's movement behind us and the pregnant teenager is with us, a plastic bag in one hand. Up close, she looks softer, more fragile, although her hair is showing dark roots and her make-up is harsh and unforgiving. She has a cold.

"Has she been bothering you?" The girl sniffs and wipes her nose on her coat sleeve. "She never stops talking."

"Mummy!" Moira jumps up and down again. "The angel lady is taking me to see daddy."

I point at my name badge apologetically, unable to speak.

"I'm sorry." She shakes her head, but seems upset. "She's too young to understand."

Again I say nothing. What is there to say? For a moment, my life had possibilities, but minutes pass and time moves on.

"Her daddy died last month," the girl continues. "Car bomb in Basra. I tell Moira that daddy's in heaven with the angels now, but she still thinks he'll be home next week."

And I wonder if I have this all wrong. Maybe I was never meant to be a mother after all. Maybe what Moira really needs is a grandma.

Eugénie Murray Golding

RIVER NILE

Fascinating River Nile,
May I talk to you a while?
Tell me of those golden kings
And sacred cats bedecked with rings.

Of rituals in days gone by
And temples towering to the sky.
Sacrifice was often done
For Ra, the Bird God of the Sun,
Tutankhamun, Rameses –
Names that never fail to please.
Scholars come from many lands
To solve the mystery of the sands.

And in those far-off olden days
You rocked a babe, the Bible says.
So turn the page of history
And please reveal it all to me,
Everything I want to know
Of Egypt high and Egypt low.
I am entranced, O River Nile,
My heart and soul you do beguile.

Debbie Mitchell

ON REPEAT

It is June.
I kick a ball
around the lawn,
careful to avoid the daisies.
Not always with success.

Under a flawless sky
a bee harvests nectar
from wild borage.
A wood pigeon warbles.
A favourite sound.

A plane flies overhead.
Next door's dog whines.
Birds, invisible in the trees
twitter on.

Outside is perfect,
vibrant and wholesome.
Inside is dying, for all I know.

Somehow, the grass looks greener,
the water I sip tastes sweeter.

I pay attention to every insect,
every cobweb shimmering in the sun,
every wild flower and leaf.
Too much to see, to leave.

It is June.
I will see you again.
On repeat.

ROAD KILL

Bill Webster

From their elevated perch the grey-cloaked figures surveyed the road below.

"This is where it happened, son. This is where the bastard killed your ma. Driving like a lunatic. Didn't slow down when he saw her. Didn't even stop when he hit her."

"I remember that morning, Da." He looked sideways at his father before returning his attention to the carriageway below, his ears straining and his beady eyes seeking the first signs of their target. He shifted uncomfortably and felt the gorge rise in his throat. "She was fussing about the little ones as usual." He gave a little nod of his head. "She was the best ma in the world, Da. And always so particular about her appearance."

"Aye well, lad. Happen as she was a sorry sight later that morning. But at least it were quick. She wouldn't have wanted to live on as a cripple." He sunk his head into his chest and was silent for a moment. "Just one second earlier or one second later, and she would still have been with us." He turned and looked at his son. "You were always her favourite, you know. She would be very proud of you today."

The son shifted uncomfortably. "I hope so, Da. Just so long as I can hold it all together for long enough." His eyes flicked down for a moment. "The pressure's really getting to me now."

Their heads twitched in unison as the sound of an engine broke the early morning silence.

"Get ready, lad!"

The noise came closer, and then a red estate car appeared sedately around the curve half a mile distant.

"False alarm, son. Our man will be going twice that speed at least."

"And black, Da? A black car?"

His father nodded.

"Use this one as a dry run, son. Watch its progress. Think about what we need to do and when we need to do it. Timing is everything."

They watched the car braking as it passed by them, losing most of its speed before negotiating the tight ninety degree corner just beyond their vantage point.

"He'll be soon now, son." The father shivered as he turned back to resume his vigil. "I can *feel* the wicked bastard coming."

"He can't come soon enough for me, Da! I feel like I'm going to explode!" He hopped from foot to foot with a determined expression on his face.

The noise of another engine cut through the stillness, but this one was much louder and sounded like the feral scream of a beast in anguish.

"No mistake this time, son. That's him."

The black hot hatch hurtled into sight and rocketed towards them.

"Remember son, timing is critical! Wait until you see the whites of his eyes!"

"Just say when, Da! I'll be with you all the way!"

"Now, Son! Now!"

And father and son moved as one ...

The ambulance left the scene slowly and silently, leaving the recovery truck driver surveying his task.

The car had been massively deformed where it had struck the telegraph pole on the outside of the bend. It had then been flipped into the air and sailed over the fence into the field where it narrowly missed a tree and now lay upside down almost fifty yards from the road.

"He must have been travelling some," he remarked to the man who was accompanying him.

"By all accounts he always was." The yellow-tabarded cop shook his head and breathed in the familiar smells of hot oil and tortured rubber. "He was on nine points. If we'd just caught him one more time then maybe this could have been avoided."

"Poor little bugger," his companion responded. "Well, silly little bugger really … but you know what I mean."

The policeman smiled and nodded, and watched as the other man looked at the car, and then back at the road, and then scratched his greasy head.

"Well, officer, I've seen a few crash sites in my time, but I can't understand what's happened here. It doesn't look like he slowed for the corner at all."

"Yeah, that was puzzling me too." He considered for a moment, and then turned back towards the road and beckoned. "Come on. Let me show you something."

They walked back along the debris trail that marked the path the car had taken.

"Just over here. The windscreen came out a bit smashed up but pretty much intact. Take a look. What do you see?"

"Shit!" the recovery truck driver exclaimed.

"Precisely. I've never seen anything like it in twelve years in traffic. It's like a whole flock of pigeons dumped on him, and I'm guessing it must have been right in the braking zone. Just one second earlier or one second later, and he would still have been with us."

They raised their eyes as two pigeons cooed contentedly in the tree above them. They looked at the birds, and then at each other, then laughed at themselves and turned their thoughts to clearing the wreck and reopening the road.

Linda Leigh

THE MOUNTAINS

You were born millions of years ago
It was cold, dark
Ice ground your stone and harsh granite
Moulded your features
Designed your face

Time made you grow tall
As more ice ground stone
Earth expanded and shrunk again
Ice pushed you upwards higher in the sky

Your face touches the skyline
Shadows cascade down
The base of your skirt touches the ground
Petticoats fling out their lace all around

Gigantic now as earth revolves on
Fire subsides
Ice has gone
Quiet repose

You lie in state next to each other
Each carved differently
Smiling gently, contentedly
We drive on by, gaze upwards to gauge your height
Try to guess your age

Standing tall once, now lying down, stretched out, peaceful
The world acknowledges who you are
And just why you were born in rage
Millions of years ago

Gwili Lewis

SOUVENIRS

I've travelled the byways of Cymru
Her mountains and valleys to view,
The beauties of Penfro and Powys
And the lakes around Elan so blue.
I purchased a plaque up in Bangor,
It pictured a wild Snowdon track,
'Cymru am Byth' was on it,
But 'Made in Hong Kong' on the back.

I heard the sweet bells near the Dyfi
And the lark rising clear in the sky.
The singing of male voices thrilled me
And a tear trickled down from my eye.
A Welsh hat I purchased in Cardiff,
One tall, shiny and black,
'Cymru am Byth' was on it,
But 'Made in Hong Kong' on the back.

Now I am happily married
And I have a charming Welsh wife,
Our garden so full of red roses
Is far from the maddening strife.
Our heir was born in the springtime,
A fine handsome fellow named Jack
With eyes like the blue skies of Tenby,
But I'm frightened to look at his back.

SECRETS

Colin Mackay

An old man sits beneath an oak tree, the breeze gently cooling his face in the hot sun. He watches the people who have come from miles around just to view the statue of the princess. They come from the various kingdoms of the land and from far across the seas just for one glimpse of the fragile perfection.

Some will stare for hours at the delicate carvings, debating the pose and expression on her face. *She is wistful,* they would say. *She is dreaming,* some say, others that she is sad. Some just want to see and admire the exquisite workmanship, the subtle lines and curves of her face and hair cascading over her shoulders. Some even throw coins into the ice-cool, clear waters of the surrounding fountain. *Such a treasure,* they say, *could only have been sculpted from true love. Hence it must bring good fortune and luck to those that make a wish to it.*

Standing in the immaculate rose gardens in the old king's palace, it stands as a tribute. Though the king is no longer there, the palace is kept in all its splendour for the visitors who visit daily to marvel at the wealth and magnificent opulence. But it is the statue and the fountain surrounding it that they will remember when they leave.

It was built from a solid block of marble, and the sculptor had spent ten years of his life working on the piece, carefully chipping away at the stone with the most delicate of touches.

He could not be rushed, harried, forced or coerced into working faster. Sometimes he would not touch it for days, weeks – even months at a time. *My hands cannot achieve perfection at this time so I cannot work,* he would say, his tears glistening like diamonds in the sunlight as he gazed upon his slowly forming masterpiece.

Now it stands in the garden and only the old man knows her thoughts, for they are his thoughts as well. *A true love,* they say, and he smiles a sad smile, for he knows they are right. It was a true and perfect love. But it was also a love that could not be. A love between royalty and a commoner. A love between a princess and a sculptor.

Lee Howell

GRAND DESIGNS

This week,
London yuppies,
Mad pair,
Kevin McCloud.

An idea,
A plan,
A foreman,
Kevin McCloud.

Late delivery,
A foundation,
Huge bill,
Kevin McCloud.

Bad weather,
Brickwork done,
Damp walls,
Kevin McCloud.

Extra loans,
Mother-in-law dies,
Child ill,
Kevin McCloud.

Silly husband,
Silly wife,
Further loan,
Kevin McCloud.

Weeks behind,
Pregnant wife,
Leaky roof,
Kevin McCloud.

Horrific weather,
Cheaper alternatives,
Wife hospitalised,
Kevin McCloud.

Broken foot,
Windows sealed,
Walls plastered,
Kevin McCloud.

Floors laid,
Electricians in,
Plumbing done,
Kevin McCloud.

Wife shopping,
Private loan,
New furniture,
Kevin McCloud.

Kitchen done,
Bathroom fitted,
Place painted,
Kevin McCloud.

Furniture in,
Flowers everywhere,
Beaming smiles,
Kevin McCloud.

House tour,
Garden walk,
Hefty tag,
Kevin McCloud.

Year's passed,
Baby born,
Sale sign,
Kevin McCloud.

Next week,
Yorkshire barn,
Sheep farmers,
Kevin McCloud.

FIVE A DAY

Les Green

This morning I'm praying to the 'Oh God!' of hangovers to leave me alone.

I lay in bed for ages needing a wee, but I wouldn't get out because it was nice and comfy and warm and not even a bit headache-y. When I thought my bladder might burst, I jumped out of bed and ran for the loo. If I'm not mistaken I think I just passed the same litre of water I'd drunk at 5am.

Exactly the same colour but a little bit warmer.

Breakfast was a cavalcade of saturated fats, carbohydrates and builder's tea. I hope I can stay friends with it for a few hours.

I just realised that I haven't showered or dressed yet so I'm sitting at the table completely naked, with a trickle of egg yolk hardening on my moobs while I try to decide whether a ciggie right now would give me a heart attack or not.

I light up anyway and immediately begin to wheeze like an asthmatic marathon runner with only one lung, carrying a wardrobe up a flight of stairs. I love smoking.

I shower with a lemon-and-lime shower gel, idly thinking that this might count towards my five-a-day. This sends me on a scavenger hunt through the cabinet to find a coconut shampoo and suddenly I'm on a mission to get through the whole five before I leave the bathroom.

1. Lemon and
2. Lime shower gel
3. Coconut shampoo
4. Mint mouthwash
5. Cucumber face mask (this was in the bathroom cabinet

when I moved in)

I pop a couple more painkillers for luck and swill them down with more mouthwash. My head should now be pain free and have a nice fresh minty smell.

I remember going into the bedroom to get dressed, but after I sat on the bed to pull my shorts on I must have fallen asleep. I woke up about 10.30 with one leg in my shorts, the headache completely gone and a strange minty freshness in my nostrils.

Alex Bell

NAVIGATION

In the darkness of life
when every road is a cul-de-sac,
every street intimidating and
violent. Knowing if you
select 'home' on your satnav
it will only return you to your
heartache and sadness.

Instead you enter 'happiness'
into the panel, in the hope
that it may guide you there,
a place you mislaid the directions
for a long time ago.
The voice states,
without a hint of irony.
'*Please* try again.'

Lowering your expectations
you prod 'contentment' into
the box, a shorter journey,
a reasonable request maybe.
Again the voice,
'*Please* try again.'

Feeling lost amongst the dust
of the demons, you finger
through welled-up eyes
the destination 'normal',
heaven is in the mundane –
for the depressive
the voice tins out
'*Please* try again.'

Out of options you
punch 'suicide' into the
machine, then put your
foot down hard –
smashing into the wall
with the words
'turn around when possible'
filling the silence.

THE HOUSE AT COLEMBERT

Liz Sandbach

The station at Colembert was cold and deserted as the young woman put down her bags and took out the crumpled pieces of paper from her pocket. She read again the advertisement that had brought her here: "Artist requires female model in exchange for free lodgings, south-west France. Apply Monsieur Grunberg, La Vergnolle, Colembert," and his brief reply: "Be on the 15.20 train. Someone will collect you."

As she stood waiting a sharp November wind blew down the tracks and through the station, trying to rip the papers from her hand. It swirled the rotting leaves around her feet then moaned through the vaulted ironwork of the roof. She shivered and felt suddenly alone. Then she heard a gruff voice say "Mademoiselle Devine?" The French pronunciation took her momentarily by surprise as she turned to see a small stout man waiting by the exit.

She smiled and answered "Oui Monsieur, c'est moi." He gestured sullenly for her to follow him out to a battered old van then threw in her bags.

They drove through the silent town, its grey streets narrow and oppressive. The only sign of life was an emaciated dog, head down, battling its way through the wind. As they headed out into the countryside the wind died down and a mist rolled up and lay over the fields with a quiet melancholy. A feeling of unease crept along her skin and although it was unsettling she welcomed it. After all, she had chosen to come here for exactly this reason and hoped that its bleak atmosphere would help her finish the last chapters of her book.

Half an hour out from the town the driver pulled up outside a pair of rusty metal gates. She got out of the van, grabbed her bags, and pushed open the gates. The garden was overgrown and she had to pick her way carefully down the moss-covered path that inclined steeply through overhanging bushes and trees. The house was larger than she'd expected, more the size of a *manoir*. With its strange unbalanced proportions and its air of dilapidation, it was an ugly house.

There was a note pinned to the heavy oak door "Don't knock, just enter." She turned the iron handle and opened the door, stepping into a large empty hallway which echoed to the sound of her footsteps.

"Hello, is anyone here?" she called, but there was no answer. An air of decay and neglect pervaded the house as she began to search for any sign of its inhabitants. There were many rooms, some locked, some open; those she inspected were sparsely furnished and ancient tapestry curtains hung in tatters at the shuttered windows. It was as silent as the grave and there was no one to be found.

She decided to try upstairs and worked her way along dusty corridors, which had many twists and turns. It was dark and gloomy, as if the house did not welcome the light. The only sound was the rhythmic rise and fall of her breathing. As she turned a corner, she detected a smell of turpentine that managed to overpower the dampness. She realised she must be nearing the artist's studio. At the end of the long corridor she noticed a chink of light from beneath a door. She knocked and waited for an answer. None came so she knocked again but there was still no reply. Slowly she turned the handle and went inside. It was a huge room with a tall ceiling and two large windows, shuttered against the evening. A massive stone fireplace at the far end crackled with burning logs and in one corner was an antiquated four-poster bed. There were paintings stacked everywhere, all of young women, some clothed, some not.

"Monsieur Grunberg?" she proffered, and from behind a huge easel someone stirred.

"Is that the English girl?" His French had the thick accent of the region and it took her ears an extra second or two to adjust.

"Yes Monsieur, I'm Jenny Devine."

"Come over here, Jennee Devine, let me see you."

She moved across the room towards the voice. "That's far enough. Stop there." She stopped and waited. Then the face of an old man peered at her around the side of the canvas. His sunken eyes were set in creased yellow skin that hung loosely from his bony cheeks and white matted hair fell onto his rough brown smock. He smelt of paint and tobacco.

"Ah yes, white skin and red hair. And blue lustrous eyes. A good combination. Sit here." He beckoned to a chair a few feet in front of him.

She sat motionless as his gaze travelled over her face and body. His scrutiny made her feel uneasy but not with any sense of impropriety – it was more a feeling of having her soul invaded.

"Yes, you will do nicely. You will sit for me each afternoon – the rest of the time is yours to do as you please. Your room is at the top of the house. Take up your luggage then come back and sit for me."

She found the attic room and deposited her bags. Then, as instructed, she went back to the studio.

"Take off your coat and hat and let me see what is underneath. Yes, that blue dress works well. Sit like that, with your hands folded on your lap and let your hair tumble over your shoulders. Yes, that's good. Now don't move and don't speak unless I address you."

He painted without stopping for what seemed like hours. She could see the flourish of his brushes and his beady eyes, intense over the top of the canvas.

"May I rest for a while Monsieur?" she asked.

"Very well, if you must. You can take a few moments to tell me about yourself and what has brought you here."

"Well Monsieur I'm from the north-west of England, from one of the salt-mining towns." She thought she saw a flicker of something pass across his eyes. "This pendant I'm wearing is made of rock crystal hewn from the salt that lies beneath our houses." She held out the crystal for him to see more clearly but he recoiled and she thought she heard him suck in his breath.

"And why did you reply to my advertisement? What makes a young woman want to be in Colembert in winter?"

"I'm writing a book, Monsieur, and I think this is the ideal setting for me to be able to finish the final chapters."

"I see. Now, let us continue a while longer and then you can retire to your writing. But first, remove the pendant; I need to see all the blue marbling beneath your skin. Do not wear it again when you are posing."

Over the following weeks Jenny fell into a routine of writing in the mornings and evenings and sitting for the old man in the afternoons. Sometimes when the house closed in on her she would go for long walks in the countryside around Colembert. And each day the weather grew colder and the winter mists rolled in off the river.

She struggled to adjust to the cold and damp and the meagre warmth that the little oil stove afforded her. At night she was kept awake by scratching sounds that she thought were mice but that Monsieur Grunberg had assured her were bats. But she persuaded herself that it all helped create the perfect ambience for her writing.

One afternoon at the beginning of January when she went to the studio the old man said he wanted to move things on to the next level.

"What do you mean, Monsieur … the next level?," she asked.

"I'm ready to paint you without your clothes," he said. "I like to slowly strip away the layers of my model until I understand what lies beneath."

She was surprised at how easy it felt to bare herself to him but she felt safe under his painterly eye. He painted her in various poses and from various angles. She liked the portraits he produced – they made her look beautiful and captured the essence of her being, especially in the depth of her eyes.

During these sessions they spoke little but while she was taking a break one afternoon he asked how her writing was progressing.

"It's almost finished, Monsieur; I'm onto the final chapter."

"And what is this book about?"

"It's about vampires, Monsieur." His eyes widened.

"And why do you come here to write about vampires?"

"Well, when I was on holiday here in the summer I found an old manuscript entitled *The Salt Vampires of Aquitaine*. The salt in the title intrigued me and the legends in the text inspired me to weave a tale. Your advertisement seemed to offer the perfect opportunity to return and finish my book in the proper surroundings."

"And what *are* these legends of vampires?"

"Well, Monsieur, the manuscript says that descendants of Dracula – or Vlad the Impaler to give him his real name – fled Romania when they were persecuted and some of them ended up in the Dordogne region where they could hide in the wooded hills and deep caves. Over the centuries these descendants integrated with the local people and intermarried and are now living ostensibly as ordinary villagers. And the only way you can tell if these people are from the Dracula bloodline is if they are afraid of salt as this is said to be deadly to them."

"And do you believe such tales?"

"Of course not, Monsieur – I don't believe in vampires. As I said, these are purely medieval legends and myths. But they make a good background for a story. Vampires are big at the moment – they've made a comeback ... books, TV, films."

"Is that so?" he answered softly.

"And may I ask you a question in return, Monsieur?"

"Go on," he said.

"That door at the back of the room – where does it lead?"

"It leads nowhere; it's just a store cupboard."

"Then why do you always lock it whenever I enter, Monsieur?"

"Paints are expensive and old habits die hard – no other reason. Now be quiet and resume the pose. I've started to peel back the layers but there is still more to reveal. I want to see what it is that makes your heart beat faster and the blood course through your veins. I want to see into your soul. That is what a great painter always aims to do – to paint what is below the surface – that which ordinary men cannot see."

But she saw something in his eyes that disturbed her. When she was lying in bed that night turning it over in her mind she knew he was hiding something. It played on her mind and every day her curiosity grew; she had to find out what lay beyond the locked door.

Some days later when thick ice lay on the ground and Jenny shivered in her garret she decided to ask the old man for a second oil stove for her room. When she got to the studio the door was slightly ajar and she knocked quietly but got no answer.

She crept inside. The old man was lying on the huge bed asleep. She turned to leave but then turned back, drawn to the door in the far corner of the room. The door was closed but the key was in the lock. She carefully turned the key; the old man did not stir. Then she turned the handle and stepped inside the room. She found a switch and turned on the light. The room was full of paintings. She looked around her and at first her eyes refused to believe what they were seeing. Then an icy terror gripped her heart and her mouth gaped in a silent scream. She trembled with fear. Suddenly the awful meaning of his words hit her and made her bowels shrivel within her: *I like to peel back the layers to what lies beneath.* He had stripped away the layers of flesh and painted the red pulp of their bodies, the heads still framed hideously by the untouched hair. But worst of all were the staring terror-stricken eyes.

She was immobilised with fear, but from somewhere deep within her came a primitive instinct for survival and she turned to flee. But he was standing in the doorway and she saw the flash of the blade in his hand. He bared his yellow teeth and snarled, "So now you know my little predilections. You people with your pathetic little stories of vampires. You know nothing. Yes, we are from the ancient Vlad bloodline but we do not grow fangs and suck blood. We take our pleasures in ways you cannot even begin to imagine. And we no longer need to hide – we are out there among you and we are many! You cannot know us – only the bats know who we are and cling to us."

He lunged at her with the knife but she ripped the salt pendant from her throat and threw it in his evil face. He screamed and writhed, spitting out obscenities in a strange dialect. She ran past him, out of the room, out of the studio and down the stairs. She wrenched open the heavy oak door and fled outside into the freezing night. Her heart was thumping against her chest and she could still hear his demonic screams.

But then another sound came, growing louder and louder, like the flapping of leathery wings. She looked up and saw a black cloud, beating and screeching as it came. There were hundreds of them, black bats with their mouths gaping and their teeth gnashing. They bore down on her, tearing at her clothes, ripping them to shreds. Then they attacked her flesh, hundreds of teeth biting and tearing. One bat clung to her mouth, covering her face so tightly with its wings that she could no longer scream. And when they had finished stripping back the layers until there was just the red pulp of the body with its staring terror-stricken eyes, they disappeared as quickly as they had come, into the night.

And as the winter mists rolled up from the river, once again the house at Colembert was as silent as the grave.

Chris Gough

SUMMER BIRDS

Choirs of summer birds call out to me.
Capturing my mind and focusing its thoughts back to you.
Their voices remind me of the pain as
your spiritual essence strokes at my heart.

Your vivid image holds solid in my dream's eye.
Your face a mask of perpetual serenity
and I catch the lingering scent of a moment's passion,
though it has long been used and spent.

You are gone, yet still you spin my world;
still you influence my actions;
still you mould my perceptions,
and I have nothing but you on my mind.

There is no symphony of angels to guide my soul.
I have no freedom to follow my passions,
I am not complete without you by my side,
and the summer birds keep calling.

FULL OF (COFFEE) BEANS

Bob Barker

"Would you like the paper?" the voice said.

About to bite into my bacon sandwich I stopped and looked up. The elderly man at the next table was twisted right round in his chair. He was wearing a plain cream raincoat and flat cap. In his hand was a folded copy of the *Daily Mail* which he was holding out toward me. The expression on his face seemed vaguely anxious, as if he had something riding on me taking it.

"Thanks," I said, "but I've got one here." I pointed down to where my tablet lay next to my plate. I only get the paper editions at weekends now.

He raised himself so he could see what I was pointing at. When he saw the flat object, he gave a disdainful look.

"Oh, I can't be doing wi' all them phony things." He turned away sharply. I guessed our brief exchange had been enough to reduce me, in his eyes at least, to the status of 'geek' – which at my age, I don't mind at all. Leaving him to his musings, I went back to my reading.

I'd first noticed him as I took my seat in the supermarket's café, looking forward to catching up on my paper's Friday film reviews over a spot of breakfast. He'd seemed agitated then, eyes casting up and down the line of checkouts, as if looking for someone. A walking stick was propped up on the table's other chair. I didn't pay him a lot of attention at the time, but I confess I probably pegged him, stereotypically, as 'frail, old Granddad', parked by some son/daughter/grandchild in the café while they did their pre-weekend shopping.

Returning to my reading I tried to lose myself once more in the reviewer's analytical dismantling of the latest blockbuster. But the man's interruption had the effect of imprinting him on my consciousness as, over the following few minutes, I became more and more aware of his growing anxiety. He kept turning in his chair, looking first this way, then that, raising himself up every now and then to widen his view. The lost expression he'd been wearing when I first saw him seemed to be moving towards panic. Watching him, a feeling of sadness crept over me. And as I remembered the odd occasion when, in his latter years, we'd parked my own father in some convenient place while my wife and I went off to 'do stuff', I felt a profound sense of guilt. Even so the bacon's lure was distraction enough that I wasn't aware of the woman's approach.

"Is anyone sitting here?"

I looked up again. The same generation as him, she had silver-grey hair, styled younger than her age, but not too much. She was dressed simply but smartly in a pale blue coat and matching scarf. The coat was open, revealing a cream top and a grey skirt. She was wearing pearls. My mother would have described her as 'well-kept'. Looming over his table, she awaited his acknowledgement. There was a slight flush to her face, like she needed a rest.

To begin with he remained lost, head still turning. Eventually he seemed to register her and looked up. "What? What'd you say?"

Hands full of shopping, she nodded at the chair across from his. "I said, 'Is anyone sitting here?'"

Following her indication, he looked at it as if its presence was a surprise. "No," he said, simply. Leaning forward he moved his stick out of the way, before returning to his distracted state.

If she found his off-hand manner off-putting in any way, she didn't show it.

"Good." She dumped her shopping on the chair. "Would you mind keeping an eye on my bags while I get a coffee?" She didn't wait for a response but headed off to the counter.

I saw him cast one suspicious glance in the direction of the bags, another at her retreating back, before returning to his search for whoever he was waiting to come and rescue him. I smiled to myself.

Old folks.

It was a good ten minutes later when I heard, "They're *so* slow here."

She had returned with a tray carrying her coffee and one of those tiny paper containers of milk. As she placed it down on the table, he squirmed in his seat a little, embarrassed it seemed by her chattiness. I just caught the brief, "Hmmph," as he carried on scrutinising the checkouts.

"Someone needs to put a bomb under them. That'd shake them up a bit."

He threw a glance her way, showing a bit more interest than he had so far, but remained silent.

"Thank you for looking after my bags."

He nodded, and turned away. I saw her brief smile as she sat down.

There was something about her busy manner and confident tone that put me in mind of a school teacher. And as she went about settling herself – slipping out of her coat, unwrapping her scarf – I saw the way she kept glancing in his direction, as if pondering his distracted state. Eventually, she reached down into one of her bags. To my surprise she took out a tablet, similar to mine. Opening the cover she switched it on. It was a little while before he noticed it, but when he did he stopped his swivelling long enough to focus first on it, then her. Eventually he returned to his scouting, but every now and then I saw his gaze slide back to her, now engrossed in whatever she was reading and her coffee.

A couple of minutes passed, then I heard, "Would you like the paper?" Glancing up I saw him offering it to her, as he had me.

She returned him a warm smile. "That's very kind of you, but I prefer to use this." She showed him her device, turning it so he could see the screen.

As he looked at it, blankly, I expected a repeat of the disdain he had shown me. But as his silent stare continued I sensed a dilemma within him. She was similar age to him, and had been thoroughly polite. Eventually he said, "What is it?"

"It's a tablet."

The blank look stayed. It made me think of how my father never liked it when my mother had the advantage.

"Would you like me to show you?"

Teacher I thought again. Definitely.

He gave an offhand shrug, as if to say, "If you like," but I saw him lean in.

Over the next several minutes, between finishing my reading and breakfast, I observed them as she ran him through the gadget's capabilities and he shuffled his chair closer to hers. At one stage she interrupted her demonstration to introduce herself. "I'm Diane by the way."

He nodded, keeping his eyes on the screen. "Russell."

She gave another, amused smile, but didn't let it linger.

I wondered how much of what she was saying he was taking in. But as the lecture continued I saw the way his gaze turned more and more to her face, rather than watching what her fingers were doing.

Eventually she closed the tablet's cover. "They're very useful. You should get one."

He nodded, but didn't look convinced. Sitting back in his chair, he started to gaze around again. But now the agitation he had shown previously was gone.

As she finished her coffee I saw her eyeing him over the rim of her cup. She seemed to come to a decision. She put her cup down.

"I come here every Friday. I don't recall seeing you here."

The look on his face was something between shock, and outright fear. Being shown something was one thing, casual conversation, another.

"I … er, I …" he stammered. "I come with my daughter and granddaughter. We're usually here earlier, but I couldn't find my key."

She gave a sympathetic smile. "I like the coffee here. Much better than Tesco."

He stared at her empty cup. "Is it?"

"Oh yes. Don't you think so?"

It was clear the question had never occurred to him. "All tastes the same to me."

Another smile. She smiled a lot. "Not if you like coffee."

He shrugged.

She rose from the chair sharply enough to make him jump. "Well I like it, and I'm going to have another. Can I get you one?"

The way he froze in his chair, staring up at her, mouth open, she might have asked if he wanted to take her to bed. "I, er … I …"

"I'll take that as a 'yes'. Sugar?"

He just managed a slight shake of his head.

"Right. Back in a moment."

She headed off to the counter. He watched her all the way to the queue. He was still watching when a young girl skipped up behind him, smiling.

"We're back Granddad."

He turned. Behind her was Mum, followed by Dad, pushing a fully-laden trolley.

"Sorry to be so long Dad," she said. "Because we were late, its busier than usual."

He smiled at his granddaughter. "S'okay. No problem."

"Are you ready to go? We've got to walk into town and call at the bank yet." She looked about him. "Where's your stick?"

"Here it is," granddaughter said, picking it up from where it had slid to the floor.

As she handed it to him I saw him glance over at the queue. The woman was next in line to be served.

"Come on then," his daughter said, hurrying. "If we leave it too late getting out of town, the traffic will be horrendous."

He stood up, a little reluctantly I thought. He was taller than I expected. not as stooped. With one last, sad glance at the queue, he turned to follow after his family, already making ready to troop towards the exit. I looked over to where the woman was now being served. Shame.

They'd moved only a few steps when he stopped.

"I think I might stay here."

His daughter turned, sharply, a trace of alarm in her face "What? Stay here? Why, aren't you feeling well?"

"Yes, I'm fine. But if you've got to walk into town I thought I might wait for you here. You can pick me up when you come back for the car. If that's okay?"

His daughter gave a suspicious look. "Are you sure you're feeling okay? Did you take your tablets this morning?"

"Yes, yes, I took them. But it's a bit of a walk and it's still raining. You'll be quicker without me."

She looked at her husband, who gave an unconcerned shrug, eager to get going. She turned back to her father. "Would you like Milly to stay with you? We don't know how long we'll be at the bank. We could be a while."

Milly pulled at her mother's sleeve. "But Mum, I've got to go to Top Shop. You said I could." Her mother looked conflicted.

He gave her the nearest thing to a smile I'd seen him make. "I'll be okay. You go and do what you have to do."

"Are you sure you'll be alright? Do you need anything?"

"No." Then he added, "I might have another coffee."

She looked shocked. "Another coffee? Dad, you never have a second cup of coffee."

"Well I will today. Just for a change."

"Okay. Sit down, I'll get it."

"No," he said, almost too quickly. "I can manage. You get off. I'll be fine."

She gave him one more suspicious look before giving in. "Alright. We'll be quick as we can."

"Take your time. No rush."

As they went on their way, he returned to his seat.

A minute later the woman arrived back with their coffees.

"Was that your family?"

He looked surprised. "Er, my daughter. And grand-daughter. She's just turned eight."

"What a lovely little girl. You must be very proud."

"Yes," he said, finally managing a smile. "We are. I mean, I am."

The woman checked him, then spent the next minute or so focusing on her coffee, leaving him to his memories.

Eventually he looked up. "Do you … Do you have grandchildren?"

She peered at him over the rim again. She was one of those who could smile with her eyes. She put her cup down. "Would you mind excusing me for a moment? I just need to use the bathroom." She rose but waited, looking down at him. There was a moment's stillness as they regarded each other.

"Of course," he said.

He waited until she'd disappeared, then he took off his cap and smoothed back the thinning hair that was a similar grey to hers. He left the cap on the table. Reaching to his tie, he pulled at it, making sure it was straight. Then he settled back and waited, watching the door to the toilets.

Breakfast over, it was time for me to go. I stood up but had to pass by his table to get to the exit. As I came level with him I glanced down and our eyes met. I gave a brief nod and what I hoped wasn't too accusing a smile. For a brief second he held my gaze.

Then he returned my nod, and winked at me.

My smile stayed all the way home and, I think, most of that day.

Iona Reid-Dalglish

LOVE'S DESCRIPTION

I couldn't find a poem on love
Which didn't babble and gabble and gush
Which cut to the core of the topic above
And revealed even a glimpse of the truth about love
All descriptions reducing that wonderful stuff
To frippery, sentiment, chiffon and mush

Why does this thing which is root of our being
Become so indelibly linked with such things
As roses and chocolate
And that fuzzy warm feeling
Discovered in the lives of those stylised beings
Imprisoned on stage, page and screen?
When in fact love grows in the mess and the woes
Of the people less pretty and the stories untold
And transforms into beauty what then becomes prose

And I have to conclude that the reason is this
Those who write about love are not in its midst
Not caught up in the throes of its fearsome embrace
As they take up the pen and put words to the page
But rather recall with their rose-tinted specs
The divinised bliss that their mind recollects
Of former romances, or fantasised hopes
Which remain past or future, but not present tense

Liz Sandbach

SURROUNDED BY THE ENEMY

Son of the Sioux
on the banks of the Irwell,
dweller of the prairie
in your white Salford teepee.

As your fever burns bright
do you dream of Dakota
and the Great Plains sweep
and the buffalo roaming?

Are you dreaming of water —
not this dirty grey river
but the great wide Missouri
and the Black Hills of home?

Do you think of your father
who ran through the burning
and saved you from dying.
Will he come to you now?

Surrounded by the Enemy
he named you that morning
and so it has been
all your warrior life.

Are you hunting with Sitting Bull
and Black Elk and Red Shirt
riding Ohitika Tashunke
with the wind in your hair?

Are you with your belovèd,
Awanata, the beauty,
or with Shinte Galeska
in the White River country?

Or are you in battle
killing Custer at Bighorn
on Last Stand Hill
looking down on the dead?

Or is the sun setting,
in your dark eyes reflecting
as the medicine man
asks the spirits to guide?

As you see the stars fading
and your young life force waning
do you feel Wakan Tanka
the Great Mystery calling?

Son of the Sioux
on the banks of the Irwell,
warrior of the plains
in your white Salford teepee,
do you hear the owl screech,
do you see the deer running,
as your tribe spurs you on
to the Soul's Water Crossing?
They are calling you home.

In the 1880s Buffalo Bill had started the Wild West shows in America, depicting the rise of the white settlers and their conquest of the Native American Indians. In 1887 Queen Victoria celebrated her Diamond Jubilee and Buffalo Bill brought his show to London and set up a showground in Earls Court where he staged 300 performances to a staggering 3 million people.

The London show came to an end in November 1887 and Bill decided to head north and bring his show to Salford where a huge arena was built on what is now the site of the Lowry at Salford Quays. The arena cost £15,000 and could seat 8,000 people with another 3,000 standing, at an entrance fee of one shilling. Bill had brought with him 100 Native American Indians, many of whom were Sioux Indians who had been responsible for killing Custer at Little Bighorn and who were now on the run from the US cavalry.

They arrived in Salford in December 1887 on two trains carrying Bill, a hundred Native American Indians, and livestock including horses, bears and buffalo. They set up camp in their teepees on the banks of the River Irwell. Then they all rode down the main street, advertising the show, called 'Buffalo Bill's Wild West and Congress of Rough Riders of the World'. It must have been an awesome spectacle.

But before the show could even begin, tragedy struck with the death of a 22-year-old Sioux Indian called Surrounded by the Enemy. He was a 6ft 7in warrior whose father had escaped with his baby son through fire and smoke during an attack by a rival tribe. It was this incident that had prompted his father to give him the name 'Surrounded by the Enemy'. Surrounded took part in the Battle of Little Bighorn alongside Chief Sitting Bull. Sadly, Surrounded died from a chest infection in a freezing December in his teepee on the banks of the Irwell.

Glossary: Ohitika Tashunke – Brave Horse; Shinte Galeska – Spotted Tail; Wakan Tanka – The Great Spirit or Great Mystery; to hear an owl screeching meant impending death.

THE WEDNESDAY CLUB

Andrew Cripps

Probably the most unusual Wednesday Club in the country; for over twenty-five years railway enthusiasts, or train spotters if you must, have met at Acton Bridge Station. The station is the last on the West Coast mainline before the Liverpool line branches off; that means all the port freight trains and the Halewood car trains pass through Acton Bridge on a daily basis. In addition, all the West Coast main line trains serving stations to Glasgow and London, as well as to Birmingham and the South-West, pass through.

Few people use Acton Bridge station, although of late the numbers have increased, maybe because London Midland has decided to increase the number of trains that stop! In its heyday, the station had a ticket office and a delightful small garden area on platform 3. Today the station is unmanned and the garden area overgrown, looking quite sad.

The club is unusual in that it has no rules, no membership or subscription fees, and anyone with an interest in trains is welcome anytime. I discovered the club when commuting between Acton Bridge and Liverpool. Now that I am retired, I attend 'meetings' whenever I can. One of my fellow commuters was met by her husband and five-year-old son most evenings. The young lad showed a real interest in trains and members clubbed together to buy him a train book to help foster his interest.

Perhaps the startling feature of the club is the number of enthusiasts who have travelled a goodly way to join the Wednesday gathering. To my knowledge we have had members come from as far afield as Halifax, Blackburn and Cardiff. Regulars travel from North Wales and the Wirral and spend many hours, often in the cold and wet. I live less than a mile away almost from the station and feel a cheat!

One ritual that amuses me is the 'take away' run! At 4.45pm, a member collects orders and money, and goes to the local chippy to buy a fried supper. This is eaten in their cars before returning to the platform for more spotting.

Members arrive as early as eight o'clock in the morning and stay well into the evening, long after the sun has set.

What is the club's future then? With better communications today, I suspect the club will grow in membership and the distance from which they have travelled will increase.

Must close now – I have a train to catch!

Corey Estensen

WAR DIARIES

(Upon transcribing pages from WWI Regimental war diaries for the National Archives.)

What surprised me most was that a record was kept at all.
Maybe it shouldn't have ...
After all, it was an officer's task to be literate, to communicate –
as well as to ride a horse and attend regimental dinners,
while the troopers and privates sweated their way
through the countdown to death.

But the trenches, although below ground, were great levellers.
These grave young men, commissioned from their schools and colleges,
exemplarily literate, painstakingly thorough,
scribing the minutiae in spidery hand, made wobbly by the
shells and the guns.
These captains of men captured
the swelling and shrinking of the body of the regiment,
carefully recording the place names in capitals.

And they, too, were taken.
When it came to casualties, only the officers were named.
The 'other ranks' were only 'dead' or 'wounded',
appraised in tonnage, not souls.

Bill Webster

THE LITTLE BIRD

The day is long and tepid
And birds are really stupid
Here comes one now
All beak and wingèd –
And flies into my picture window.

O little bird what have you done?
Your little life is squandered
Against my plate glass picture window.
(Which came as part of a super deal
From Atkinson's Double Glazing, Rochdale.)

But hark! My little wingèd friend is stirring –
He was not dead but only dreaming
Of nests and eggs and clouds and breezes.
(But not of cars or boats or cheeses
Which are of no interest to a little starling.)

Farewell my little wingèd friend!
Fly, fly, fly, fly, fly away –
And pray desist from coming another day.
But fly instead into someone else's glazing
And leave me in peace with my picture window.

THE OLD GAMEKEEPER

David Bruce

It wasn't one of those wealthy shoots like the Duke's lower down the moor. In fact it was probably the poorest shoot in all of Yorkshire. So high was it that the heather was slow to sprout and what with this paucity of food and the extreme cold, the birds inevitably drifted lower down to his lordship's beats. There wasn't even a decent track up the moor to the shoot and it was a two-mile soggy tiring foot slog to get to and from it from the road.

John and Peter had inherited it from their Uncle George seven years ago, along with his large and prosperous farm in the valley. Uncle George had been a very generous and a kind uncle to the boys. But despite being a canny Yorkshire farmer, or should that be tight-fisted, he had social ambitions. He wanted to be able to boast about his grouse moor and so he'd bought just what his inbred nature dictated. The cheapest and inevitably the poorest shoot on the market, sitting and exposed right on the very top of the moor. Going shooting up there onto their uncle's prized piece of moor was like making a pilgrimage for the boys. A pilgrimage they willingly made in memory of their dear uncle.

In the first few years the shooting had been fair. They had the benefit of a part-time keeper – old Charlie. He'd retired as his lordship's head keeper but he was born to the moors and liked to keep his hand in. Charlie was a widower living in a little grace-and-favour cottage on his lordship's estate. Apart from his cottage and the moors the only place you'd find Charlie was in the bar at the Golden Fleece. He'd sit in an old wing chair by the fire, smoking his pipe, and blowing the smoke up the chimney, but really he was half-asleep most of the time. Old Charlie had disappeared over three years ago now. They'd tried his little cottage on the estate and almost the whole village had come out to search for him on the moors, even his lordship had joined in, but Charlie had never been found.

John and Peter had had a long day on the moor. The grouse had been sparse and the shooting poor. Nothing new there then. Then as they began to descend, the clouds swept in and the rain began to hammer down like icy steel rods, as they trudged and stumbled through the wiry heather and slippery peat. They rushed to get clear of the exposed hillside as thunder and lightning followed the beating rain. Their two spaniels seemed immune under their thick wiry coats. They were still scurrying on ahead, noses down, still scenting, almost lost in the coarse rank heather.

Suddenly there was a loud yelp and a whine, and one of the dogs started to bark. The lads rushed forwards. Peter's dog Sue had slipped into a pot hag; one of those steep-sided pits in the peat with the fetid dark water swilling around in the bottom. The dog was trapped, it was deep and the sides too steep and slippery for it to climb out unaided. Peter leant in over the edge, grabbed the dog's collar and began to pull her up. It was then he first saw the whitened bones sticking out from the walls of the hag. There was nothing particularly unusual about bone in a hag wall. Many a sheep fell into a hag and died there, but then a flash of lightening glinted off something much brighter. A slim golden chain was hanging free from the peat wall.

John heaved the dog up onto the bank and then leant back down to look at the chain. He pulled and one end came free from the soft peat. There was a little gold pendant hanging from its end. Another pull and the other end came free with a gold hunter pocket watch hanging from it. Peter stood to show it to John. They both looked at it in surprise. Then Peter wiped the watch with his sleeve and there engraved upon it were the initials C.H.C., Charles Harry Cotter, the initials of their old friend Charlie, the long-missing gamekeeper. Surprise turned to an understanding and a sense of great sadness at the thought of how their friend had ended his days alone up here. They prayed that his end had been quick, perhaps a heart attack, up here on the moors he'd loved so well.

To mark the spot they built a little cairn of lumps of peat and the few stones they could find. Then they said a few words over their friend and hurried from the hill and the storm.

They were on the moor the next morning with the police constable and two ambulance men struggling with a stretcher through the heather. The remains were recovered and brought down to the village. A week later Charlie's remains were laid to rest alongside those of his wife and ancestors in the little cemetery close by the village church.

After the service the men all took to the bar in the Golden Fleece, reminising with tales of Charlie's exploits, how he'd chased them off the moor as boys and how he'd helped them in their manhood. They'd already drunk several toasts to the old gent when Peter happened to glance across to the wing chair that Charlie had always called his own. There was a figure sat in the chair or at least it seemed so, for the only real light in that corner came from the flickering fire in the inglenook. He looked again even harder and he could see a hand and glass were raised, and as Peter hesitantly raised his own glass in return the image began to soften and weaken until it was just a swirling cloud of peat-dark dust that swept across the hearth in the inglenook and was drawn up the chimney.

Old Charlie was finally on his way.

Les Green

MOVE DOG, MOVE

Move dog, move. Get down onto the floor.
You're always in the way when I'm opening the door.
You always get there first and you know it's not for you.
What goes on in doggy brains to act the way you do?

Move dog, move. Get down now off the bed.
This is where the human sleeps so get it in your head,
puppies don't have pillows, puppies don't have sheets.
So get back in your own bed and let me go to sleep.

Move dog, move. Stop getting in the way.
I want to watch the telly and you always want to play.
You chewed up all my socks again – not funny any more –
so go and get a doggy toy and get down on the floor.

Move dog, move. Don't do it on the floor.
You've played out in the garden so don't you scratch the door.
When I try to clean it do you have to chase the mop?
I'm tired of all the puddles. Won't it ever stop?

Move dog, move. I've told you this before.
You always want what I want and there isn't any more.
Chocolate's not for doggies but maybe if you sit –
try and be a good girl then you can have a bit.

Move dog, move. I'm opening the tin –
just another second before you cram it in.
No one's gonna steal it. It's right there on the floor.
You haven't even finished and you're looking round for more.

Move dog, move. Come over here to me.
I can easily watch the telly with your head upon my knee.
I can stroke you on the snout and scratch behind your ears.
And we can do it every night for a hundred canine years.

WALLPAPER

Marian Smith

It was late when the removal van left and we were exhausted. Our bed was still in pieces so we laid a mattress on the floor and unpacked sleeping bags; I sent Toby to the takeaway we had spotted on our way into the village.

The Old Vicarage. We had wanted it as soon as we stepped over the threshold. How often we thought that it would slip out of our reach during the slow, grinding conveyancing process. A house untouched by DIY enthusiasts, it had not been tainted by fitted wardrobes, UPVC windows or an imitation gas fire. The last occupant, an octogenarian, had lived there all her life and had treated progress as an intruder to be repelled at all costs. We didn't want to change anything. We would refresh, repair and renovate but leave the soul and heart of the house intact.

Now, alone in the house for the first time, I wandered from room to room, touching the old oak wood panelling in the front parlour, the ornately tiled fireplaces, the cast iron range in the kitchen and the grain on the banister as I climbed the stairs.

I felt the warm glow of optimism. This was our future. Already I could see family around the vast trestle table which we had bought for a song because it was too heavy to move. I could hear our unborn children shouting in the garden, a Christmas tree in the corner of the parlour beside a fragrant wood fire; the sun streaming through the lattice windows into our bedroom which overlooked an abundant vegetable patch with its bean wigwams and tidy rows of onion tops and cabbages.

I turned on the light in each bedroom; the glow from the naked bulbs was cheerless and stark. Each room brought different emotions; plans and ideas jostled and elbowed for attention. My footsteps echoed on the bare wooden floors, as if the house was calling out, waiting for us to take possession.

The rose wallpaper in the back bedroom was perfect but old and faded. In the front bedroom, the pale lemon stripes were bolder and brighter where a wardrobe had protected the wallpaper from the early morning sun, but almost bleached to cream elsewhere. We would find the closest copies so we could repaper both rooms.

In the bathroom, an old Victorian pine washstand stood in the corner, pushed aside with the advent of internal plumbing. I stroked the knotted wood, gently wiped the dust from Victorian tiles to reveal forget-me-nots entwined with honeysuckle.

Finally I pushed open the door of the smallest bedroom. The nursery; instinctively I touched my belly as I walked inside.

Something was different in here, changed from our last visit – a room at odds with the rest of the house. It was the wallpaper over the mantelpiece. Why hadn't I noticed it before – had it been concealed behind a large picture or a mirror, like a scar hidden from view? I would have remembered, for it was the ugliest wallpaper I had ever seen. Creeping ivy, nettles, bindweed, on a blood red background.

It would have to go.

As I drew closer I saw that a corner of the paper had come away from the wall. I smiled to myself – I couldn't resist this small act of benign vandalism. I pulled it and it came away easily; perhaps whoever put this wallpaper up must have known it was destined to be removed, because once that was done, another came loose, first in small pieces no bigger than a beermat, and then in larger strips.

It was only after a few minutes that I saw words or parts of words beneath. The writing was in capitals, it was childlike, in pencil, scrawled. First the word HE then U' then FLO – it could be Florence or Flora – perhaps written by the old lady when she was a young girl.

A few more pieces of wallpaper fell onto the hearth. Then the word ALL was revealed.

I was conscious of a crunching on the gravel outside and the car door slam. Toby was back with a takeaway. But I couldn't stop tugging at the paper; a fragment of the cottage's personal history was about to be revealed – I had to read the rest of the hidden message.

A large piece had come loose from the plaster beneath and as I pulled a great strip of paper came away. I stared at the wall, and stepped back as if I had been burnt. The future fell away from me.

TAKE UP THE FLOORBOARDS. ALL OF THEM.

Nick Monks

WINNEMUCCA, NEVADA

I stood in the cold, coldest snow.
The gambling isles were not for me.
The bandit lights and tunes were left-alone fun –
Sierra Nevada, Alps, Andes – three ways
to spell and taste mountains.
There was a McDonald's – there usually is –
so I had a coffee and toast with egg, poached.

Elsewhere is a childhood room I've left.
You, the reader I don't know, Anne sitting in an eternal armchair
in an eternal garden with the treacherous kitchen.
These are the places that give Winnemucca, Nevada
its presence and placeness.

If I could add up the snowflakes of Winnemucca
something may be discovered that is close to love.

The pioneers headed west into California, Washington:
to be different I pioneered east.
You see I was four, eighteen, sixty years old:
memory is as important as the today.

This anti-cowboy is heading to New York
without a horse or revolver except by simile,
making a study of different ways to say goodbye to places.

TO LONDON. WHAT A PITY!

Gwili Lewis

Over the years I have been many a time to London for a
weekend, to see a theatre show, or to sing in choral festivals in
the Royal Albert Hall. Then on the Sunday before returning
home, tour the city, having a good look round the main tourist
attractions, with a well-informed courier providing too many
facts for me to take in. Sometimes a leisurely hour or so gave
sufficient time to have a meal.

The last weekend visit to the big city was in 2004 when a
group of us from the Northwich Welsh Society went down for
the Massed Male Choir Festival. Just think of the thrilling
sound of 800 male voices. The choir from my home village
was there on stage. But I didn't know this until I bought a
programme. I had been a member of it fifty years before.

What shocked me was to note that the vast majority of the
choristers were either white haired or bald. Many were well
over 80, the majority over 50 years of age and the youngest was
18. What a pity. So what is the future going to be for Welsh
Male Voice choral singing?

But to return to London. If at all possible, whenever we're
in the city, we always try to visit St Martin-in-the-Fields in
Trafalgar Square, not only for a quiet time of contemplation
and prayer, but also to have a meal in the crypt. I have never
been in a busier eating place. No wonder, the food is good and
wholesome with generous helpings. What makes the place so
fascinating for me are the customers, from all parts of the
world, and some dressed as if they were in their homeland.

In 2004 on a wet Sunday, my wife and I sat comfortably at
the table, said grace and were about to start our meal, when we
saw a middle-aged man, bearded, barefooted, enter down the
steps from the rain outside and walk to the tables which had
not been cleared. His looks reminded me of Jesus. He was

obviously poor and hungry and ready to eat other people's leftovers. Then one of the staff approached him, took hold of his elbow, and led him to the steps, out to the windy wet streets.

What a pity! I felt terribly guilty, and on reflection should have bought him a meal.

I couldn't help thinking about a one-time vicar at St Martin-in-the-Fields, one I'd heard a lot about when I was young. Reverend Dick Sheppard, a lovable man, generous and extremely popular, one who battled relentlessly for the poor and the hungry during his ministry. Unless I'm very much mistaken, it was he who pioneered the use of the crypt as a refuge for those desperate souls in need. I wonder what his reaction would have been if he had been a witness to what I saw.

Singing in the Royal Albert Hall, even with a few hundred others, was a never to be forgotten experience for me after retiring in 1981 to Pencoed, near Bridgend in South Wales. The Pencoed and District Choral Society wasn't a big one, but it was noted for its 'beautiful sound'. On our return journey from London we sometimes stopped at Windsor for a meal.

I'll never forget one occasion during a bitterly cold spell. In such wintry weather, it was wise for me, an old age pensioner, to wear long johns for essential comfort on that London trip.

Rushing to dress in the London hotel that icy cold morning, ready for the homeward journey, I felt quite pleased with myself that I had indeed packed my long johns. When we arrived at Windsor, we were all looking for the public convenience. Well, such was the effect of the cold weather.

There was a real problem for me … my long johns were back to front.

What a pity!

Joan Dowling

YESTERDAY

I shivered with the excitement of it all,
beside myself with hope and possibility.
That longed-for scarlet dress –
a fifteenth birthday wish come true.
The satisfying staccato of adult heels –
a statement of my new maturity.
My unruly hair surrendering for once
as if rising to the occasion –
and the audacious crimson lipstick
echoing the promise of the red dress.
Luminous eyes looked back at me
from the unfamiliar mirror.
Was that really me?

A taxi.
Usually just for weddings and funerals.
My two best friends waiting at the dance hall,
solemn faces suppressing nervous giggles.
Coats discarded in the cloakroom,
each admired the others' finery –
but secretly thought their own choice best.
We hovered breathless in the doorway,
held spellbound by the lights and music.
Then, last-minute cries of panic –
Don't leave me on my own! Never.
Holding hands, we pledged allegiance
and crossed the threshold to our first grown-up dance.

Was that really fifty years ago?
It feels like yesterday.

Won 1st Prize in the 2013 Swanwick Summer School Annual Poetry Competition.

LIKE SHIPS

Colin Mackay

He bounds the steps up to the station platform, breathing heavily in the cold winter air, just in time to see the train approaching from the slowly thickening mist. He sees that there is only one other person on the platform, a woman with a Costa coffee cup in her gloved hand, long brown hair underneath a grey woollen hat. He sees that next to her is a very large suitcase. The train pulls into the station and after an alarm beeps, the door slides open with a hiss. A few people get out and continue on their journey into the early evening gloom and he sees the woman is now struggling to get the case onto the train. He walks quickly over to her.

"Allow me," he says.

"Thank you," she replies softly.

Grabbing the handle he lifts the case on to the carriage after the woman has got on to the train, storing it safely in the luggage area at their end of the car.

"There," he says. "All done."

She smiles, nods, but says nothing. They both look down the carriage to see that there appears to be no empty seats, instead face after face looking at them with pity. Looks like you are both standing, at least until the next station, they all seem to say.

"Standing room only then," he says.

The train moves away, slowly at first but rapidly gaining momentum and the man and woman stand together but apart. There is a jolt as the train switches from one set of rails to another and the woman falls back slightly. Instinctively his hand comes up to stop her falling further.

"Are you alright?" he asks.

"Yes fine," she replies. "Didn't even spill any of my coffee."

"Wouldn't want that."

"Far too precious. It's the one rule I have. Never to spill any of my skinny latte."

"I can see how much it means to you," he says.

They fall once again into a silence only punctured by the sound of the train.

There is an announcement over the tannoy. They will soon be approaching the next station.

"My stop," the woman says.

"Would you like me to help you with the case?" he asks.

"Thank you. That would be nice."

The train once again slows to a stop and the doors open. The woman gets off and the man steps off with the suitcase. As he hands its over to her, their fingers gently touch and their eyes make one last contact. She smiles shyly and he finds himself doing the same.

"Thank you once again," she says.

"Don't mention it. Hope you get home safely."

"And you."

The man jumps back on the train as the doors slowly close.

As the train once again pulls away from the station, he watches as the woman pulls the suitcase along the platform. As she disappears from view he wonders if he will ever see the lady with the skinny latte and shy smile again.

Valerie Sullivan

BUTTERFLY BRIDE

She flitted across the summer lawn
Cabbage-white fragile
Delicate steps across the green
Long-limbed, trembling
Dipping to kiss nectar from her guests
A matronly rose, full-bosomed and blown
A shy, retiring orchid hiding behind
A cheerful sunflower, golden light and loving
A dowager buddleia, aged and bent and chairbound.

She bent to kiss the dowager on the cheek
Her veil folded in like opalescent wings
Took a last fragrance from her bouquet
And laughing she raised it over her head
Tossing it high in the air
Excitement lifting the 'oohs' behind her.
She dipped to sip nectar from her wine glass
And turned to see that Sunflower had won the prize.
Another summer wedding, then.

Alex Bell

SHADE IT BLACK

How did the remains of American servicemen and women get from the dusty roads of Fallujah to the flag-covered coffins at Dover Air Force Base? Jess enlisted in the Marines immediately after graduating from high school in 2001, and in 2004 she volunteered to serve in the Marine Corps' first officially declared Mortuary Affairs unit in Iraq. Her platoon was tasked with recovering and processing the remains of fallen soldiers. Yet they received very little support afterwards. Jess Goodell's book, Shade it Black: Death and After in Iraq.

Across the gunfire, beneath a truck,
flashes light up my collection.
The explosion has done its job,
Oh God, how it has done its job!
I must do mine.
They say we are trained,
there is no training to prepare you for this ...
Same boots, same belt,
it could be me, it could be me.
I wish it were me.
His pain over, mine just begun.

I freeze.
Feeling inept I lie there motionless. What do I do?
I do nothing, nothing.
A nearby shell shocks me. I start clawing out
at the burnt meat, grabbing all I can see ... all I can smell.
Quickly, quickly, get this over with.
No fear. Pure anger.
Body bag partly full I drag myself out.

The Unit greet the old me. She doesn't exist.
She was left behind in the cold shadow of the truck.
Congratulations on a successful mission
Got there before the enemy. Job well done.
I ignore the high five ...
The light falls upon the open bag.
They are also quiet.

A half-finished jigsaw,
the marine lies on the table.
We stare at the spaces the bomb has left behind.
I shade these in black on the paperwork.
The inventory begins.

His pockets full of life,
Rules of Engagement neatly folded,
scrunched up trash that didn't become litter,
a picture of smiles from his high school football team,
a half-full bottle of Blue Star ointment
and
from his bloodied breast pocket slips a sonogram of a foetus.
The silence now louder.

DETRITUS

Debbie Mitchell

I reside by the roadside.

Here amongst the waste, the rubble, the junk of humankind.

I live in the bushes and the scrub and in between the tall, hairy-stalked weeds with their jagged leaves and piss-yellow flowers. I watch and I wait. I am unseen but I see you as you pass by at 60, 70, 80. Any speed you choose, regardless of the signs. I sit in the back-draught and I see you. I see the detritus you throw from open windows and I know you. I know you by your waste.

Here come the smoker, the drinker, the compulsive eater. Fag ends still glow and spark as they suck in the oxygen in their dying moments from window to ground. They burn me before they turn grey and die. A vodka bottle offers its dregs in a spray of clear drops before it shatters into a thousand shards, piercing me as they fall like rain. A half-eaten burger smeared with bloody ketchup with fragments of bread-skin clinging to the meat, lands in the gutter like road kill.

I am alone here, yet never lonely. I am occupied. Rummaging. Tearing. Harbouring. Ripping. Shredding. Devouring. Your unwanted fills my needs. Up to a point. But I am always waiting for the big one. The main meal. I am patient. I can wait. Will my reward come from the city businessman in his blue pinstriped suit, his mind half on the road as he closes another deal on his hands-free? His sleek black car sends up a spray of gravel as it speeds by. The remnants of his brie and grape ciabatta mix in with the dirt, and satisfy me. Up to a point. But not enough. I wait for the big one.

There goes the lorry driver, thundering by, drowsy from an illegal eleven hours on the road, a trail of chocolate wrappers and empty paper coffee cups in his wake. He shakes with the caffeine that keeps him from sleep. Behind him a distracted mother drives with one hand on the wheel, the other shaking a rattle to stop the child from crying. Baby on Board the notice in the rear window proclaims. Don't drive close. As if a baby on board makes a difference to the tailgaters. The blue car passes by; the plastic sack filled with soiled nappy and tied with a knot, a reminder that it came this way.

There goes the tourist. The off-duty nurse. The man in the white van. The newspaper hack chasing his story chewing frantically on gum, wrappers forming a silver paper trail along the road. The flashing lights of a speeding ambulance. The red and black leather-clad motorcyclist leans towards me as he takes the bend. But he doesn't see me. None of you see me. But I am here. I reside by the roadside amongst the plastic bottles, the unspooled cassette tape, the crisp packets, used condoms, supermarket shopping bags, newspapers, torn pages from dirty magazines, batteries, banana skins, apple cores. All human existence is here.

I see fleeting glimpses of the lives of the owners of this refuse on their faces. Behind-the-glass expressions of joy, worry, abandon. Of lust, anger, frustration. Thoughtful, confused, greedy.

The 17-year-old boy in his first car, souped-up with spoilers and chrome. Baseball cap back-to-front, soft down on his face, he feels like a man, looks like a child, drives like a lunatic. Empty bottles of alcopops and candy wrappers bounce and flutter and fall beside me.

Forty bus passengers, with forty stories and forty offerings of rubbish to be offloaded anywhere along the route. The young hairdresser in her pink car filled with pink fluff and a pink sticker telling us 'hairdressers do it with a hairbrush'. What will be her gift to me? Pink bubblegum to seal my lips?

A moment of quiet now. A break in the traffic. A gentle breeze ruffles the wrappers and packets, whistles like the sea-surf as it caresses the empty bottle necks.

I am hungry and I wait. I wait for the big one. The main

meal. I slither and crawl among the garbage. Endlessly patient.

The asphalt rumbles as more of you approach. Here come the group of ramblers in their Volvo. The illicit lovers. The stony-faced middle-aged couple who sit in silence, nothing to say. The child molester. The wife beater. The hippies in their campervan. The illegal immigrants crammed into the back of a truck. The farmer and his horse-box. The football hooligans throwing out bottles of urine. The priest. The school kids, off on a day trip. All of humankind – in its innocence and its guilt, passes me by. Leaving remnants of itself.

The sun begins to sink behind the clouds and the sky turns to blood and now my reward draws near. The silver saloon slows to a crawl and pulls off the road, its hazards flashing the colour of discarded orange peel. The engine cuts out, the driver's door opens. I froth and salivate. He's a salesman, tired and overweight and drenched in sweat. His hair is greying at the temples and his eye bags are bloated with cortisol. His dark flannel trousers are creased and his gut stretches the fabric of his shirt, gaping at his belly to reveal ashen flesh.

He opens the bonnet and looks despairingly at the metal inside – neatly crammed together like a space-age city. He stares at the car's innards. He unscrews caps, he jiggles wires, he taps the engine, twiddles with the carburettor. He doesn't have a clue how this hunk of metal works. This four-door saloon which comes with the job, a job he hates. No commission today. None yesterday. And now this. Broken down in the middle of nowhere. He fetches his mobile phone and dials, but it runs out of power. He swears out loud. The sweat drips from him. He has an appointment in half an hour. This one looked promising. An old lady. Cash and vulnerability a-plenty. Easy pickings.

The salesman reaches inside the car and fumbles with a blister pack of tablets, popping three and taking a swig of water from a near-empty bottle. He finishes the last of a bacon and tomato sandwich and throws the wrapper to the ground. Then he takes a final gulp of water and casts the bottle into the bushes. He doesn't see me. He doesn't know I'm here. He thinks he's alone standing by the side of the road with his broken down car and his broken down life.

I have gorged on your trash, but still I am hungry. Hungry for the big one. And here it stands, unsuspecting. Unlike the spindly jogger who came this way last week – all bone and tight muscle, spitting globs of germs onto the roadside – this one is meaty and blubbery. My feast awaits. I slither and crawl and move in for the kill.

I reside by the roadside and I feed off human detritus.

SERENDIPITY

Joyce Ireland

They can be magical moments. There are four wonderful bronze horses that prance above the great west doorway of San Marco in Venice. But they are replicas. The originals prance in a high gallery behind them. We climbed up to this gallery on a quiet day when there were fewer people than usual in the square. The horses are magnificent and almost perfect after hundreds of years out in the weather. My companion walked on, round a corner in this L-shaped room and I was completely alone with the beasts. The sensation of movement as they reared up in front of me was dizzying. I felt as though at any moment they would gallop away, through the cathedral, out into St Mark's Square and away past the Doge's palace.

I imagined I could hear them snorting as they rose, hear the clatter of their hooves and the rush of warm air, smelling horsey, as they escaped down the stairway, manes streaming and through the great door, scattering tourists as they thundered past.

Then others entered the gallery and the spell was broken.

Nick Monks

BEPPU

I came from Kyoto's gardens and Osaka's traffic, Mount Fuji.
The green mountains taste like sweet, sunless, damp moss,
the sort of blue Rothko paints, the sea, a Gauguin sky.
Fishing boats and nets, lobster pots, harbour walls.

The hotel would only let me check in, the room was available
at 2pm,
as is the custom in Japanese hotels,
so I wandered the small town for four hours disconsolate, hurt
even.
Tried to climb one of the mountains, but couldn't: got sunburnt,

asked the sea why I was always alone and was this good or not.
To which she answered truthfully you're not.
So I am now thirsty in the middle of Beppu, adding up objects
to try to make infinity.

Elsewhere I count three Stars of David on arty Christmas trees;
in the thirty visits to the park
eight benches, two McDonald's, five pretty women, eighty cars.

Christmas day was a day of aloneness,
a quiet and peace that tenuously vibrated in the air –
a sort of not-Christmas, that made it more so.
A pleasurable Christmas.

Now, having a room in a town of fishermen and Christmas lights,
a place of conditioned cool air and a stillness without clocks.
Trying to climb mountains of syntax and logical equations
with mere, small love.

Liz Leech

WALKING IN WIRRAL

Children fly kites high on cliffs
Above the Estuary of Dee,
And tumble down through tussocks
To a pebble-strewn edge of the sea.

Knots, oystercatchers and turnstones
Forage the tide line with questing beak,
Ebb tide flows, exposing Wirral's shore.
And time is fleet, is fleet.

Silver-scaled salmon are back
As waters become clean,
And rumours abound of otters
Reinhabiting the river upstream.

Now, just remember the past
As you gaze out at the sea
To when Roman and Viking
Bore down to conquer with glee.

Or when during the Restoration,
Cheshire cheese won renown,
Ships carried it past these headlands
Bound for London town.

And eighteenth century Irish folk
Paced Parkgate for passage home
With help from fair wind and tides
To sail past Thurstaston.

With history so rich
And nature so fair,
Don't you just wish
That you could go there?

ROAD TRIP TO LUXEMBOURG

Les Green

I was working in Belgium, and, like all other European countries except us, they celebrate their bank holidays on the day they fall. They don't move them to Monday or Friday in order to have a long weekend like we do.

On this occasion it fell on a Thursday and everywhere in Belgium was closed – and that includes the office we were based in – so we piled eight people of mixed nationalities into two Vauxhall Astra Estates and went on a road trip to Luxembourg.

On the way there we stopped at Waterloo so Gary could say that he'd been. It was little more than a field with a hill in it but Gary seemed to enjoy it. The Italians just scratched their heads and exchanged puzzled glances with our Portuguese and Mexican colleagues. If only we'd thought to invite some French friends!

We all went up the mound. Grainne and I got up last because we stopped half-way for a ciggie and we couldn't breathe any more. We walked around the top pointing at distant Belgian fields and a quad bike track for a while. Nobody took any pictures because we'd all left our cameras in the car and it was hardly worth doing all those steps again. After we all got tired of pointing, we descended the mound and got back in the cars and, after a brief exchange of ideas over a rubbish map we found in the glove box of one of the hire cars, we drove off in the direction most of us vaguely believed was the way to Luxembourg.

As we zoomed out of Waterloo, I spied a gift shop on the corner that was selling French, British and Belgian flags. As we slowed to turn onto the main road, I saw some small models of Napoleon, standing erect with a hand tucked behind his back. I wanted to see a model with him scuttling away with his tail between his legs but that wouldn't have been good for the tourists. I looked as hard as I could in the few seconds it took to join the road but I didn't see any models of the Duke of Wellington.

C'est la vie!

We soon discovered that a bank holiday in central Europe had no similarities to a bank holiday in the UK. Everywhere between Belgium and Luxembourg was closed. Well not everywhere. We found a newsagent so all piled in to take advantage of the generous Luxembourg rules on taxing tobacco products. We then went looking for something to eat.

After walking around for ages we found a hotel but they only had a bar and nowhere to eat. When I asked them why they didn't have a restaurant the manager said it was because of all the eating establishments that could be found in the city. I said that we found them too, but they were all fucking closed.

Eventually we accidentally stumbled upon a Pizza Hut. And it was open! We all scrambled inside like seagulls fighting over a cold chip and squeezed six people onto a table meant for four. Hold on … six? There should be eight … the Italians were missing! One of us was sent out to look for them while everybody else got stuck into the menus. The messenger came back with the news that the Italians would not be joining us. They felt that they would rather go hungry than to eat pizza, pasta or anything else from a Pizza Hut that claimed to be Italian.

So, with bellies full and carrier bags stuffed with cheap fags, we went back to the cars and began the drive back to Belgium – the classic rock emanating from the Dutch language radio station intermittently accompanied by the rumblings of two empty Italian tummies.

Bill Webster

RIDING HIS ULTIMATE WAVE

He's riding his ultimate wave,
carving a path to perfection,
tracking into a watery cave
and speeding into oblivion.

Carving a path to perfection,
calling surfer joy to the sky
and speeding into oblivion.
But look at the glint in his eye.

Calling surfer joy to the sky
as the reef races inches below.
But look at the glint in his eye
as he cuts to go with the flow.

As the reef races inches below,
the wave sucks and coral-heads rear.
As he cuts to go with the flow
his mind is consumed with the fear.

The wave sucks and coral-heads rear.
Tracking into a watery cave,
his mind is consumed with the fear
he's riding his ultimate wave ...

Lee Howell

NUCLEOCOSMOCHRONOLOGY

Lyman-alpha forest, so green in its depth.
Silicate minerals colliding, into criss-cross crystals.
Moenhopi flying southwards in a glint of an eye.

Super-massive, purple abiogenesis in a cauldron mix,
extrusive, siliceous, oozes to the time of music.

Redshifts pattern downwards, tired of light.
Spheroid halo dances in the wide-open court.
Coccolithophorids, milky-brown, wrap around trees.

Acidification, furrows grey pearls of wisdom;
fluvial fruits dance on tired light.

Mega-parsecs blunder on the hard, wet floor;
photometry twirling in the twinkling night sky;
sedimentation unfurling with a thermal flux.

Surficial regeneration of the optimal splendour,
chasing hydrocarbons in the salinity of peace.

DAUGHTER OF LIR

Debbie Bennett

There's a keen wind off the cliffs tonight. Banshees wail in harmony with the mournful cries of the seagulls that circle above the waves. The tide is in too, a rhythmic pounding on the rocks – the sea's heartbeat growing stronger as the hour approaches. There is a feeling of anticipation in the darkness; lives have changed, battles been won and kingdoms lost on nights such as this.

Standing on the headland, by the edge of the crumbling chalk with hair stinging his face like a thousand tiny insects, he waits and watches as he's waited and watched for what may be a hundred lifetimes. If he closes his eyes, faces the wind and looks with an inner vision, he can see forever out there in the ocean.

But it's not forever he's looking for. Not tonight with the memories strong and the image of her so clear in his mind it's as if time itself has looped back for him, giving him another chance to reach out for her, hold on to her and keep her as he's kept her love in his heart for so long.

Aisling is her name. Daughter of the Gods and forbidden to one of his kind. Aisling, who came to him on a night like this and left him with such a longing that life became meaningless without her. A sea vision, the sailors said – a child of the ocean sent to snare mortal souls with such beauty and song that could charm the angels from heaven itself and make them seem pale shades, ghostly silhouettes against the spell of the children of Lir. Superstition and yet he believes, for he can hear her now, hear the haunting melodies in the wind and the sea.

There is a power in the song, and power still in the singing.

But his Aisling has no need of such weapons. He is already under her spell and willingly. They have pledged their love for one another and though he knew her time was short, he has her promise to hold onto. And when her father called her home, she swore to return one day, to love him as only a child of the Gods can love.

So each year he waits on the headland and listens to the voices of the sea, secure in an unearthly love for a woman who is not mortal. Each year he listens for the song and hears only the banshees' cries, premonitions of a death for which he can only dream until he finds her again. For the love of a God carries the price of eternity and he knows he will never find peace without Aisling.

The wind stills to silence. The tide ebbs. There is magic in the air tonight.

Aisling? He dares not look, but forces himself to step closer to the cliff edge. Down below, wet sand shimmers in nacreous light. The sea has withdrawn, exposing rocks like black teeth, the mouth of the ocean come to swallow its prey. Behind the rocks something moves, glistening in the shadows and he can make her out now, a slim figure in a pale shift, her hair like seaweed dressed with pearls. She is watching him, one hand touching the rock, the other outstretched towards him, pleading with him. She can come no further; Lir will not allow it. This is as far as she can keep her promise and it is not enough.

There are tears on his cheeks now, as he knows he cannot see her again. She has risked much already. But how can he live, knowing they can never be together? He sighs. *Take me with you.* He has no need of speech. She will hear him, if she chooses.

A flutter in the air around him and suddenly there are swans. Four white birds fly above him, majestic in their splendour. Slender white necks outstretched, they circle him for some moments, climbing effortlessly only to swoop down, then rise again. Up and down, round and round, until he is dizzy with exhilaration.

Aisling! There is joy in him as he knows the waiting is over, the promise kept. Yet still the swans circle, as reality crashes back in with the boom of the sea against the cliffs below. The wind howls again, the savage and ancient anger of a God defied. Aisling has betrayed her father by falling in love and he will not give her up lightly.

The swans are flying away from him now, buffeted by the wind. And then they are gone, white arrows speeding out to sea. His body shrieks with the loss, a part of him ripped open and exposed to the wind and the night. But this time it is different; now he knows he can fly too, that all he has to do is believe.

Five white swans soar high above a deserted headland. She has stolen his soul, taken what she laid claim to all those years ago and he is no longer human. And if he is no longer human, then he is free.

PORTRAIT OF AN UNKNOWN WOMAN

Tom Ireland

On the wall of an ancient library hangs a portrait of an unknown woman. She sits at a table, holding an orange. At her feet sits a black dog, gazing at her.

Lord, this is boring. I'm not made to sit still and gaze gormlessly into the distance. What? Yes, I know I'm made to gaze, but purposefully; there has to be a reason. What reason? Well, food, of course. Meat. Meat is food, I don't gaze for seeds. Oranges are just that, seeds. Everybody knows that. Who eats seeds? Birds. Vegans, maybe insects? I don't know. I'm the world's fastest animal. Well, I'm the fastest one I know. I'm certainly the fastest in this village; that I do know. Well, apart from that hawk, but she cheats. Gravity does it for her – just folds her wings and falls. I could do that, off the church tower. Expect I'd beat her – I must weigh more.

Look, what's this all about? You get the world's fastest animal to sit and gaze at a seed? Do you realise how uncomfortable it is for me to sit on my tail like this? No, of course you don't. I'm a gaze hound. Gaze hounds don't gaze at seeds. Show me a hare or a rabbit or a cat or a lion and I'll gaze at it. I'll do more than gaze – I'll hunt it down for you, chase it, tire it, kill it. Honestly, a seed. It's demeaning, that's what it is. I've got cramp in my bottom. I'm supposed to look elegant. I can't look elegant with a cramp-frozen bottom, can I?

This woman in red? Well, if you must know, she's designed for sitting. Look at her. She could sit all day and be happy; it's her talent. You gave her a cushion to sit on. She may even have a good reason for sitting on a cushion, holding a seed. How should I know? But, with respect, could she do what I can do? Can she run a hare down and kill it with her teeth? Well, I've never seen it done.

Seeds aren't good for your teeth, you know. Nothing to gnaw on. I don't see the reason for seeds. Give me a good marrow bone. I'll look at that, no problem. I'm a gaze hound, I am ...

Alex Bell

HANGING

Where do I hang this perfect picture?
I have tried the wall in the garden, the one
that catches the morning sun, but also the north wind.

I have tried the wall on the beach, the one
in the shade of the palm, but exposed
to the salt air.

I have tried the wall in the woods, the one
protected by the willow, but at the mercy
of the life that dwells there.

I have tried the wall in the park, the one
close to the laughing children, but too close
to the spray of graffiti.

I have tried the wall on the moon, the one
underlined by Armstrong's footprints, but
invisible to the naked eye.

I have tried the wall of the church, the one
in view of the righteous, but out of sight of
the sinner.

I have tried the wall in the hospital, the one
in the ward where you were laid, but a stranger
lies there now.

I have tried the wall in your room, the one
we made love against, but it still holds
the silhouette of you, hanging.

Tom Ireland

SOONLY, I

Soonly, I will do that thing with hands;
Hands and the thin stick that blackens
The white, yes, the white flat stuff who
Crinkly speaks, no, not speak. The thing
The white flat stuff that wraps, yes, and
Takes messages. Good, good, is right.
Soonly, I will do that thing. I will
Take or steal – no, not steal. Steal is
Wrong, very wrong. I know that.
But how, if not steal? Will they,
Will they, this is not fun you know,
Will they, I cannot
Find the saying thing.
Maybe I will try again after the now time.
The clock is empty now.

IN THE FORESTS OF THE NIGHT

Tonia Bevins

I found Peterson in the bar. He was up for it as usual with his perma-tanned complexion, knock-off Rolex, the crumpled linen safari jacket slung casually over one shoulder. He leaned on the counter, swirling a sundowner around his glass. Despite the chill from the air-con, I was sweating and pressed an ice-cold bottle of Tiger to my forehead. Screeching, whooping, croaking sounds emanated from the tropical night beyond the verandah. I didn't want to know...

"Bet that's them," said Peterson, his heavy-lidded gaze following two women as they click-clacked towards us across the marble. "Leave the redhead to me, Boyd, old son." I believe he actually winked and tapped the side of his nose.

They couldn't have been more different. Over dinner I found Alma sensitive and surprisingly well-read. I liked the way she smiled easily at my attempts at humour. Peterson and Felice seemed to hit it off too. She watched his every move through steady, kohl-rimmed eyes that gleamed amber in the candle-light. Laughter exposed neat white teeth as she tossed back her mane of fiery hair. On the tiny dance floor she dug her long nails into the flesh of his back as she curved her sinuous body against his. Very intimate, very fast. Peterson rolled his eyes at me and shrugged theatrically as if to say "Totally helpless. What can I do?" I thought he meant the woman. Visions of his once vivacious wife and a procession of sullen female colleagues edged into mind.

Alma and I were discussing the mystic poets when the duty manager came over to say I was wanted at Reception, a problem with our onward travel. When I returned ten minutes later Alma seemed agitated. "Your boss, my friend – they tell you goodnight. You understand? And I must go now."

Good old Peterson, I thought, a little enviously, as I turned in.

I slept fitfully and late. No sign of him at breakfast. I called his room. I knocked. Still no response when the concierge banged on his door before reaching for her pass-key. His safari jacket was on the floor, a long rip down one sleeve. The great white bed, swathed in gauzy mosquito netting, looked like a bridal fantasy but the sheets were slashed, blotched bright red. Peterson lay naked among their shreds, curled, foetal, lacerated from head to toe. I could see he was dead. There was no trace of Felice but a rank, feral odour lingered in the air and the deep green shade of the jungle seemed to creep ever closer through the open screens.

Bill Webster

NUMBER NINE LOVE SONG

Lace panties on your washing line
Red and flimsy, blew my mind
You and me could have been so fine

When you moved into number nine
A passion for laundry I did find
Lace panties on your washing line

I so much wanted to call you mine
And lie with you, our limbs entwined
You and me could have been so fine

Your nether garments made a shrine
And to their loss, you were resigned
Lace panties on your washing line

But indifference served to underline
That to my needs you were quite blind
You and me could have been so fine

Your warm blood mingles with mine
Our love by violent death defined
Lace panties on your washing line
You and me could have been so fine

Liz Leech

GLASS

The window glass was old
not rolled,
but blown, distorted,
made in times untold.

It showed the world with a different face,
distorted in size,
making views appear
somehow out of place.

Birds became monsters
on the sloping meadow beyond.
They looked huge as bustards
come down to drink at the pond.

Like life, the view proved
nothing was as it seemed,
nothing real,
only dreamed.

Yet beside that very old
pane of glass
was one brand spanking new
of another class.

Smooth and shiny,
putty still wet,
it resided where once
another was set.

Through it you could define
every blade of grass
and pigeons reduced to normal size
took wing and flew up into clear blue skies.

The choice is yours
through which to look –
to see reality or life
as in a story book.

Or perhaps turn your gaze inside
to the pier glass hung on the wall,
see yourself as you are –
or perhaps not at all.

Nick Monks

PRAGUE

The slip of day into night into day, neon sun
like a pre-war Paris or London or Berlin –
regal, pretty sash of a river,

regaled, sumptuous, majestic
mirroring the city's one hundred spires, its majesty, its presence.

In the centre of Wenceslas Square I stand and turn 360 degrees,
they're lighting candles on statue steps –
I don't know why. But it seems apt and welcome,
for all of us a vigil.

I am inside the buildings, outside/inside history,
inside a city yearning. Crossing Charles Bridge, seeing the
Hradčany castle,
I think of Milan Kundera and the Prague Spring poets.

I see Kafka's house on the far bank, 22 Golden Lane
off the River Vltava. The house he could not live in
A wilderness of thorns and unassuageable distances,
a stick insect hanging from a ceiling, taunted by family.

These buildings are Gothic, sandstone, alluring, Romanesque
and others,
deserving a beautiful river and 1000 bridges.

The more I walk, the more I am glued back
like a jigsaw puzzle, the pieces scattering in a diaspora,
rejoined like alder leaves in spring.

The English stag revellers are jokey and insouciant.
At the bus station I talk to a girl
who speaks no English. Finally I give her my loose change
before a coach takes me to Wroclaw, Poland

and the dark, demure raven-girl, ice-black hair
waves endearingly goodbye from fingertips
as I head off into Poland. Something to return to perhaps ...

Liz Sandbach

SWAY ME

Yes ... now bare my shoulders.
Brush them with your lips.
Let loose my hair
then put your hands upon my hips
and gently sway me in the candlelight.
Let's pretend we're young again tonight.

CHILD OF WAR WITH FRUIT

Liz Leech

The hedgerow was alive with birds. They chattered and quarreled as they plucked berries from hawthorn bushes and pecked holes in the last of the apples that remained on the wayside trees.

The sound of birdsong filled the air. They had come back to the gardens and hedgerows, now the corn had been cut and gathered in.

Light shone with a slanting September brightness, turning the autumn shades of the woodland into a fiery furnace. Bright red berries, hips, haws and little pebbles of bright green crab apples, scattered on the woodland floor, discarded, forgotten, forsaken?

The child had been sent out to collect fruit from the medlar tree. *Blettched*, they called it, when the little fruits, near rotten, become fit to eat. He knew where the tree was, he knew what it looked like; he had been there before.

Last year on the edge of Worcester town, with Royalists hopes gone and the young uncrowned king fleeing for his life, he had found another youth under the medlar tree, with flies and carrion dancing attendance. His face had been blettched like a medlar, with lace to wrap it around. Even a Roundhead would not have found such fruit so sweet.

Medlar, he did not wish to meddle there again, but he had never told his mother what he had seen that day. He never could.

So, he walked on humming a brave song, swinging his basket to ward off memories as he went a-gathering.

CHUFFING TRAINS

Mark Acton

I hate chuffing trains. Especially in rush hour. You think, this'll be great, I'll get loads of writing done; I can sit down for an hour or so and scribble all my wonderful genius ideas down uninterrupted.

But you forget.

You think it'll all be fine. After all, it's summer; if the train's late you can stand at the station in the glorious sunshine and listen to all those glorious summer songs on your mp3 player. But you forget that the left ear doesn't work and the right one keeps popping out and swinging back and forth across your chest, as if to say: "You can't catch me!" And you forgot to charge it.

And you also forgot that this was summertime in Britain – not in Spain or L.A. or somewhere. And that means rain. And you didn't bring your coat. Because, after all, it's summer and it'll be too warm. But it's not. It's freezing. How can it be this cold at this time of year? Why do your cheeks feel like someone's slapping a wet fish across them? Why do your arms look like they're covered in turkey skin? And why have your toes got frostbite?

And why's the ticket machine not working?

And you think, at least it'll be warm on the train when it comes. If it comes. But it's not.

And you just sit there wondering whether or not you'll have to have your toes amputated and how that'll affect your ability to walk afterwards. But at least you got a double seat. Loads of room. You can put your bag down next to you, get out your note pad and write the next chapter of your novel. And it will be brilliant. Amazing. You are definitely going to get published when it's finished. Can't wait for the film. All you need is an idea; a little spark of inspiration.

So you just play a quick game of Angry Birds on your phone. Or two. Maybe three. But then, that's it. Back to work.

Then the person in the seat in front of you turns round and stares over the back of her seat and stares at your pad and says: "What are you writing?"

"Nothing."

"Is it a diary?"

"No, it's nothing."

"Is it a story? What's it about?"

"Um."

"Can I read it?"

"I've not finished it."

"I don't mind. Let me seen what you've done."

"Um, I'd rather not."

"Go on. I won't laugh."

"It's meant to be funny."

And there's no way out. You can't say no, because you're too weak, and you know that person is going to be right there, right in front of you, staring at you and pestering you for the next hour. So you give in. You hand over your precious notepad, the repository for all the inspired musings of your artistic brain, and it's snatched away by the germ-soaked hand of a strange sociopath, who's been coughing and spluttering constantly since you got on the train. And now she's coughing into your pad. And you can see the glimmering spots of spittle glisten like glitter on the page. And you know she can't read your writing and even if she could she wouldn't be able to understand your elegant prose and poetic turn of phrase.

"You have very neat handwriting," she says. "Very small." Which is her way of saying: "I wouldn't buy this rubbish. What does it mean?" And you just want it to be over. You just want your pad back so you can get on with writing. How much of this is she going to read, for God's sake?

"What does that word say?" she asks.

Oh no, not that word, any word but that word. Why did you give her the chuffing pad? Why couldn't you just be a bit more assertive?

"Worker," you say.

"Oh! That's an 'r'," she says. "I thought it looked like an 'n'. I thought it must have been 'wonker', like Willy Wonka or something. But that didn't make any sense."

"It still doesn't make sense, you mentalist!" you think. Of course, you don't actually say anything because you're scared of her. Too scared even to ask for your pad back.

"It's very good," she says. She's lying. She hasn't got a clue. You feel a bit arrogant for thinking this but you don't care. At least you've got your notepad back. Now you can get on with writing in peace.

Until a woman carrying three bags decides she wants to sit on the seat next to you. And she looks down with disgust at *your* bag on *her* seat. And you know it's finally time to give up. You put your pad back in your bag, turn to face forwards and tuck your knees up against the back of the plastic chair that the mad woman's sitting on, put your bag on your lap, and sulk.

And then the crazy lady turns to the bag lady and says, "This young man's writing a book, you know. You should read it. Why don't you let this lady read what you've written? It's very good."

Liz Wells

PATTERNS OF LIFE

The interesting patterns that life weaves,
twists and turns, no chance to breathe.

Some people come into your life in the most unusual way.
You take day-to-day living for granted, come what may.
They touch your soul as you'd never expect,
awakening deep-rooted senses that are hard to accept.

Paths cross back and forth, zig-zagging through time,
days filled with comfortable nothing makes the soul shine.
Cherish the ones who make you feel bright,
humour, respect, times just so right.

Liz Sandbach

HOPE

The trees sighed softly like a lament
and in the deepening shadows as a vixen called
he felt the first teardrops of his loss
fall onto his sorrowful face.
All was silence in the garden of his youth.
Nothing stirred. It was as though his life – all life –
had ceased. But away from his blinded eyes
in the depth of the greenhouse
a plant put forth a shoot.

THE TWINS

Joan Carter

Thinking back, Bee realised that even Ruth's first question had been bizarre: "Do you have any children?" while everyone else was talking about food.

Bee had blinked, a rabbit in the headlights. "No, but I look after other people's. I'm a nanny." And from that reply on it seemed Ruth had adopted Bee as a confidante, addressing her almost exclusively for the rest of the evening, while the other people there had seemed determined to end the conversation. It had taken all evening for the astonishing reason to emerge.

It had been her first dinner date with Paul's friends, even though he and Bee had been dating for a few months. Bee had worried that he was too sophisticated for her, Paul being a university lecturer ten years older than her, and she'd started thinking he was reluctant to be seen out with her. Not usually concerned with immaculate grooming, more the type to sit on the floor with the kids, she made an effort. New dress, strappy high heels and even had her nails done professionally. She looked the part but still doubted that she could keep up with the academics if they started talking intellectually.

But they had all been friendly from the start. The host Rob and hostess Penny greeted her warmly when she and Paul arrived at their house. Laughed and asked, as everyone did, how she came to be called Bee, taken her coat, admired her dress.

Penny got her a glass of tonic water "I know you won't have anything stronger till you've eaten. Very wise."

Bee was surprised that Paul had talked about her. She was introduced to the two guests, Sal and Greg, who had already arrived and they all chatted, not about their work but ordinary life things and she could join in easily.

The arrival of the latecomers had been the first moment of

awkwardness. When Ruth and Ian walked into the sitting room everyone went quiet except that Bee was saying: "Yes I liked the look of him straight away," so her comment soared across the room loudly.

Paul had laughed a bit too raucously, saying "Thanks Bee!" and she had blushed, feeling stupid.

Penny had led Ruth and Ian over to her, said their names and "This is Bee, short for Beatrice, Paul's lovely girlfriend." Ian nodded with a polite reserved look but Ruth gave her a beaming smile as she took Bee's hand gently in both her cool, dry hands.

"Bee," she said, "that's a great name." She made careful eye contact with Bee, but gave a vague smile as she looked around at everyone else. She seemed frail, birdlike. Her manner had a brittle nervousness about it. Ian looked tense as he guided Ruth gently to an armchair. Sweet man, Bee thought. He's really looking after her.

Penny announced it was time to start dinner. As Bee followed the others into the dining room Paul pulled her aside and whispered: "I meant to tell you, Ruth hasn't been well for years. She's a bit, y'know," and he raised his eyebrows. "Don't take too much notice of what she says, just let her talk."

Bee could only think to say "Ok."

Bee sat opposite Paul. Ruth chose to sit beside her.

As they started on the soup Greg was talking about food he'd tried on trips abroad. "I think crocodile was the most disappointing really."

"Tastes like chicken!" Paul and Rob shouted together.

"Well we aren't having crocodile today, you'll be glad to hear," laughed Penny. She asked people to pass their soup bowls. "Next course is duck."

"Ooh lovely," Bee said. "My favourite!"

Penny beamed at her. "I know," she said, and winked at Paul.

That's when Ruth came out with it "So, do *you* have any children?"

Bee had answered: "Um, no ... but I look after other

people's. I'm a nanny," and, from politeness, had added: "How about you Ruth? Do you have any?" Bee looked over to smile at Paul but he was looking dismayed. He minutely shook his head.

But Ruth had put her hand on Bee's arm, drawing her attention and answered "Yes, I have two. Twins!" She smiled and her face was suddenly transformed, glowing.

"Oh, I always wanted twins," Bee said. "One of each and only one set of stretch marks."

"Yes," smiled Ruth. "I had one of each. I was very lucky". Then she turned away. "That was lovely soup Sally, can I steal the recipe?" She smiled broadly around the table.

Bee looked around. People were looking awkwardly at each other and seemed embarrassed. Ian, who had been looking tight lipped, drew in his breath, raised his glass and toasted "Sally's lovely soup". Rob jumped up quickly and went round with the wine again.

Sal helped Penny collect the soup dishes and followed her into the kitchen. Bee took a look at Paul's unhappy face and picked up the soup tureen. She'd clearly upset him.

As she got to the door of the kitchen Bee heard Sal say: "I can't believe Paul didn't tell her about Ruth and the twins! How could he be so dense?"

Penny answered "Perhaps we should?"

Sal said: "No they are ..." (her next words were lost as she closed a door loudly) "... his responsibility."

Bee tapped on the door. "I've brought this."

"Thanks, Bee. In the sink please," said Penny. "Actually Beatrice, it's best not to encourage Ruth to go on about the twins. It's complicated."

Bee was stunned. Penny calling her Beatrice, as if she was a child who had done something wrong.

Penny continued "Paul should have told you about Ruth and her children before you got here."

"Why? Are they ... um ... his kids?" Bee asked.

"Oh, Bee!" said Sal. To Bee those two short words sounded sympathetic, apologetic and condescending.

The kitchen door opened and Ruth came in. "Penny dear, can I do anything? I'm the only one not helping."

Bee looked at Ruth. She could hardly believe Paul had an affair with her. How horrible of him not to tell her before they got there! Did Ian know the children weren't his? He'd certainly reacted badly when she talked about them, not like the doting father of twins.

"I'll go back now" Bee said, smiling thinly, trying her best to compose herself as she went back to the dining room.

Paul was inside the door and caught her hand as she walked in. "Did the girls tell you?" he whispered.

"Yes. I know, thank you," Bee said coolly.

"Are you all right Bee?" he asked.

"Yes. But you should have told me and let me choose whether to come," she hissed. "I feel like a fool!"

"Of course you're not a fool, I knew you'd cope with it. Never mind, you know now," he said, giving her an apologetic smile.

Bee couldn't believe his nerve. She avoided eye contact with him and pushed past to her seat. She was going to see the meal through as well as she could, let him take her home and then she would tell him what she thought of him. She took a long drink of wine. She didn't care now if she got pissed. It would serve him right. She had to get through the evening somehow.

"I'm so very sorry," said Ian quietly as Bee sat down.

The poor man. His wife had children with her date but he was apologising for it. That should have been Paul's job.

"No, not your fault. I'm sorry. I've only just been told," Bee said.

He insisted: "She shouldn't talk about them. It's so awkward for everyone. But it's difficult, she's really not well."

Rob said loudly: "Let's all have some more wine eh? Get us all a bit mellow." He put his hand on Bee's shoulder and gave her a conspiratorial smile as he refilled her glass.

Sal and Ruth came in with trays of vegetables and Penny brought three roasted ducks on a massive platter. Bob carved and served duck on to plates, everybody helped themselves to vegetables. For a minute or two people talked loudly again about the food and how lovely it all was.

Then Ruth started again. "The twins are eleven next week, starting at big school after the summer."

Bee couldn't believe how shamelessly Ruth was rubbing it in. "Really? How nice" she said as if she was interested and completely unconcerned. The wine was starting to make her feel warm, relaxed and hazy. Suddenly Bee didn't care anymore. To hell with the whole rotten lot of them. "Perhaps you could tell me all about them Ruth, from the beginning."

Paul dropped his knife loudly, Sal and Penny both gasped and Ian started to choke. Ruth patted him firmly on his back until he recovered and then continued talking. Rob started topping up everybody's glasses.

Ruth smiled broadly and two spots of pink flushed her cheeks. She did look disturbed. But if she needed to talk, Bee would let her. She told Bee every detail about the pregnancy, how huge she'd grown, the difficult start to her labour, and how in the end it had to be a Caesarian birth because the twins were getting weak.

"But it worked out alright in the end didn't it darling?" she said to Ian. He bit his lip and looked down at his hands. Bee felt guilty for helping Ruth to prolong the agony of him being cuckolded.

But Ruth didn't seem to notice that he hadn't answered. She patted his arm. "We had our lovely, perfect twins, didn't we? Lauren and Laurie." She looked into Bee's eyes and carried on detailing the minute particulars of each child's feeding, colic, first smile, first tooth, first word and first toddle.

When she got to the first day of school, with Bee nodding and saying "Aah" in appropriate places, Paul said quietly "Bee, can I see you outside for a minute please." It was only then that Bee noticed no one else had eaten much. While she'd concentrated on her food, her wine and the face of this woman who was relaying every detail of her boyfriend's illegitimate offspring, the rest of the party had sat in an awful silence.

Bee decided to ignore Paul. If he was embarrassed that was his problem. She didn't care anymore, the alcohol had seen to that. Bee took another drink of wine. To her shock and embarrassment Paul got up, walked round the table and gripped her arm.

She got up, saying "Excuse me," to everyone. She could feel her cheeks burning as he frogmarched her out of the room and along to the sitting room.

"What the hell are you doing?" Paul shouted.

"How rude of you!" she shouted back. "What will everyone think, you dragging me out like that?"

"They'll all understand. I had to talk to you," he said very quietly. "I thought you understood that we don't let Ruth talk about the twins. I thought the girls had told you."

"The girls!" Bee shouted. "They're older than me and I'm not a child! Yes I heard what they said. You should be ashamed!"

He looked puzzled, "Ashamed? What do you mean?"

Bee raged on: "'We don't let her talk about her children', how dare you! Fancy bringing me here to meet the woman who you had a fling with, and who's had your children and not telling me. And her poor husband! How can he stand socialising with you ever!"

Paul took a step backwards, mouth open. "No Bee, that's not it!" He sat down hard on the arm of the armchair, shaking his head. "I never had a fling with Ruth! How did you get that idea?"

Bee snapped: "I worked it out in the kitchen and when I asked them, it was obvious from Sal's response. She spoke to me like a teacher, as if I was a child making a fuss about nothing."

Then Bee stopped and let herself hear what he had said. "What? You didn't have a fling with her?"

"No, of course not. Ruth has got real problems, she's ill. Really ill."

"Oh, Paul. I'm so sorry!" Bee was appalled at herself. She walked towards him to offer a hug but he put up his hand to stop her.

"Bee, it's not your fault. The sad truth is the twins didn't come through the difficult birth "lovely and perfect" the way she said. The thing is … she made up the whole perfect life thing, and she repeats and updates it all the time. Do you understand?"

Bee thought. "Yes, of course, how sad," she said. As a trained nanny of course she knew what he meant. The children were disabled because of their difficult birth but Ruth couldn't cope with the truth so she made up their pretend life. It was tragic. They probably lived in a home or with foster carers. Bee had cared for some disabled children during her training. They had been lovely but incredibly hard work. She imagined that looking after two disabled children at home would be about impossible.

There was a knock on the sitting room door and once again Ruth interrupted a conversation. She pushed open the door and said "Penny is about to serve dessert. It looks lovely, a gorgeous crème brûlée. Are you all right Bee?"

"Yes, I'm fine," Bee said.

Paul said: "I'll just pop back, I need a word with Rob."

"Excuse me," Bee said to Ruth and ran to sit in the loo until she calmed down. She splashed her face with cold water. When she went back into the dining room everyone was chatting about their holiday plans. As she sat down Ruth looked up and smiled, slowly and carefully eating her pudding. Bee smiled back but then focused on the food. When they had finished, Penny suggested they went back to the sitting room fire and said she'd make coffee.

As soon as Bee sat on the sofa Ruth sat beside her. She continued her account of the twins' life, describing their first day at school and how she had cried, their art projects and school outings, the holidays and birthdays and Christmases. Bee blanked herself out and smiled politely, believing the whole tale to be lies, imagining the twins in their foster home and feeling increasingly sick at heart. She couldn't wait to go home. Penny brought in the coffee.

Ruth fell silent as cups were handed round. She checked that everyone else was busy talking. "Shall I show you a photo?" she whispered, "It's the latest one of the twins." She put down her cup and unclipped her handbag.

Bee waited to see the picture. They were probably cute, Ruth and Ian were both good looking people. Perhaps they did live at home after all. At least Ian had stuck around. A lot of men with disabled children didn't, Bee knew. Ruth handed Bee the picture and she looked at it. But it made no sense.

"These are your twins?" Bee asked.

Ruth nodded proudly.

Bee looked again and tried to think of something positive to say. "Sweet," she said eventually and handed the picture back to her.

Ruth looked fondly at her children and tucked the photo back into her purse.

Bee managed to say: "Excuse me, I must pop to the loo."

When Bee left the room, Paul was right behind her. "I saw your face," he said. "She was showing you the photo wasn't she?" He had a look of the utmost sadness on his face.

"Yes. And I don't get it," Bee said, "I thought they'd look … disabled. But they're tiny! Is it a genetic condition?"

"No," he said. "I'm so sorry I wasn't clear. The thing is … Ruth's twins didn't survive the birth."

"What?" said Bee. "They were …"

"Stillborn. Yes. But Ruth's never accepted it. She spends most of her time making up whole lives for them. For the last eleven years. It must be hell for Ian."

"For both of them really," Bee said. "It's heartbreaking."

Paul wrapped his arms round Bee. "Are you up to coffee? Everybody will understand if we just go. You've been through hell tonight and it's my fault. I should have told you the whole thing before we got here."

Bee pulled away from him, wiped her eyes and stood up straight. "I know the whole thing now. If that poor couple can cope with living it, the least I can do is cope with hearing about it."

He took her hand and squeezed it and they walked back into the sitting room together. Ruth stood up and looked at Bee when she walked in. Her face held a look of appeal and hope. Bee walked across to her and took her hands. "The photograph of your twins is beautiful," she said. "You should feel proud you had them." They shared a long hug.

"Let's have our coffee now," Ruth said, "and talk about you."

Alex Bell

MONOCHROME

Really he wasn't dead, though in his heart it was said he had died
with the spurn of a lover, at least that's what I read.

– Red

Although not deranged, strange voice in head screamed
he would have to change, re-evaluate, rearrange.

– Orange

Imagine Hell on Earth not Hell below, emotions all on show,
had to survive, force himself to be mellow.

– Yellow

No disgrace in crying, but had to be seen to be strong,
big man in this scene, but not the man he could have been.

– Green

Broken hearted, broken man, broken down. Drowning in
his own shadow, desperately needing lies to be true.

– Blue

Over, just wants it over, searching for ashes of gold
in an undertaker's pot. Leaving nothing but his ego.

– Indigo

Wanting to die, monochrome arc cuts the sky, each shade
darker than the last. Leaving loved ones to regret.

– Violet

Vale Royal Writers Group

CENTO

Everywhere is quiet but for the plash, plash
of oars. A swooping owl hoots.
Silhouettes of trees soar through midnight inkiness,
the river full to the brim, the wave
sucks into a watery cave.

We'll not set false lights tonight nor flares
to lure in ships to our shifting sands;
no laden New York packet, no brig from Demerara.

In sandstone tunnels far below we await the coming storm.
The moon flickers, celestial candlelight;
only the shadows are inhabited by ghostly fugitives, Jacobites,
and us, silent souls playing cat and mouse with the Revenue Men.
Finders keep their pickings on these wild shores:
casks of rum to roll to Mother Redcap's vaults
and a sugar hill glistening among the dunes
for children to lick and spit the salt
come morning.

On its muddy way, racing, running
the Mersey talks too much, saying:
Sorry. Forgive us. Let's start again ...

Then the real journey begins.
And I will think of still waters, sacred places,
birdsong blown on the breeze and the sea
washing clean the beach and children high on cliffs
flying kites above the estuary, tumbling
down through tussocks to a pebble-strewn edge,
mudflats exposed by ebb tide where Wirral's oozing shores
greet knots, oystercatchers, turnstones.

I hear rumours of otters on the river upstream
and songbirds, joyous, fill the air; a chorus
of croaking toads answers from their pool.

I shiver with the excitement of it all,
beside myself with hope and possibility.

Over and over the spirits rise.

This communal poem was written for Wirral Festival of Firsts 2013

AUTHOR BIOGRAPHIES

Mark Acton claims that the reason he put his underpants on the outside of his trousers was that he was fighting crime. He is a liar. Don't listen to him. For this and other reasons, I suggest you do not read his work. It's rubbish. It will make you feel unclean.

Stephanie Acton is known for her down-to-earth and honest style of writing. Sainted in 1653, she was a gentle soul who, still to this day, has cauliflowers committed to cheese in her honour each year on the 31st February. All hail the Cake. Woof.

Bob Barker: Ex-cop-turned-crime novelist, it took Bob a while to realise that the last thing fans of the police procedural genre want is endless 'procedure.' Born Liverpool, lives Cheshire, a hideaway in Cyprus helps him focus on the drama and to cut out the boring bits! Helps chair a certain writing group's meetings, now and then.

Alex Bell, originally from Newcastle has lived in Cheshire since 1986. Only taking up writing in 2011 when joining a local poetry class he has had poems both published and read out on the radio. Now studying for a Fine Art Degree at Staffordshire University he regularly uses poetry, prose and text as inspiration for his pieces.

Debbie Bennett tells lies and makes things up. Sometimes people pay her for it. She mostly writes dark and gritty crime thrillers and claims to get her inspiration from the day job – but if she told you about that, she'd have to kill you afterwards… **www.debbiebennett.co.uk**

Tonia Bevins, sand-grown in Blackpool, has lived in Northwich since 1981. She worked at the BBC and later as an ESOL teacher. She's had a handful of poems published in magazines. She enjoys – and is terrified by – performing at open mic events. She wishes she could play the saxophone and juggle instead. She helps organise VRWG's Wordfests.

David Bruce. A lapsed technologist and technical writer. Now a writer and storyteller, telling his own material in storytelling clubs, for charity and anywhere there is a sympathetic audience of any age. The great store of folk tales and myths from around the world often provide his inspiration.

Joan Carter is a prolific reader who hopes one day to write a decent short story. This is her first published attempt.

Joan Dowling, retired and living in Cheshire, was one of the founder members of VRWG in 2003. The novel she started to write about that time is still a hopeful work in progress. However, having discovered she can complete a short story, she now concentrates on them – even managing to get a few published!

Corey Estensen joined VRWG in 2012. She has lived in the North West for several years after a southern upbringing, and now appreciates the views of both sides. Having written plenty of non-fiction in her employment, she has not written or published fiction since her student days; until now.

Chris Gough joined VRWG in 2003, and published his first collection of short stories and poetry in 2007. Exceptionally insightful, Chris was invaluable to the Group when it came to planning events, running meetings or providing feedback on reading. Although Chris later moved away to marry his childhood sweetheart, he never stopped taking an active interest in writing and in the Vale Royal Writers. Tragically he suffered a cardiac arrest and died surrounded by his family in February 2014 aged just 50.

Les Green is a keen writer, but claims he is better known by his pen name of 'Anon', under which he insists he has written many well-known songs, poems and toilet graffiti. He also claims to have invented swearing while on a drunken week-end in Llandudno, and is quite fond of a nicely browned pie.

Lee Howell now lives in Cheshire: is a member of four writing groups there; attends college for creative writing; has a phobia of spiders and is especially fond of cats. She has had a few articles published in **www.altblackpool.co.uk** and created a blog at **http://budbin.wordpress.com** Lee enjoys writing and is currently working on her first fantasy book.

Joyce Ireland still lives with the same husband she has had for the past 55 years; born in Lancashire, now living in Cheshire, she mainly studies and writes about the history of North West England, factually and fictionally. Favourite writing place: Gladstone's Library, Flintshire. Favourite writing tool: fountain pen. Favourite fuel: white wine.

Tom Ireland: Still living, avoiding paid employment, writing with cake, befriending mosquitoes and blogging at **gambiaGOES.blogspot**. World title – the only failed jelly-juggler in Malinding village.

Liz Leech has lived in Cheshire for the past twenty-six years. Trained in Fine Art & Design, a painter and gilder by profession, she's the writer of the odd poem or short story in between designing the flyers for VRWG's biannual Wordfest events held at the Blue Cap.

Linda Leigh has always been passionate about writing and loves nothing better than putting pen to paper, or jumping on the laptop to empty brain of creativity! Now she's retired from the day job, she's looking forward to being able to pursue her dreams, make them come true and be able to complete her lifelong ambition of writing a book.

Gwili Lewis is 93, a bilingual West Walian, a one-time library assistant who in 1949 switched to civic entertainment, serving in Cardiff and Ebbw Vale, before coming to Northwich as manager of the Memorial Hall in 1961. He has written talks and sketches for radio as well as articles for national magazines such as *Evergreen* and *People's Friend.*

Colin Mackay is 38 and has been attempting to write something decent for the past couple of years. This is the first time he has been published. He is also waiting to be picked up by a large blue police box and whisked away for an adventure in time and space. He is also single, so if there are any unattached ladies reading this ...

Debbie Mitchell is a prize-winning best-selling author, who has homes in Cheshire, London and New York. She speaks five languages, sings like an angel, and fits into size 8 jeans. And she daydreams a lot.

Nick Monks lives in Preston. He studied philosophy at Hull University and spent about seven years working and travelling around the world. He's been published widely in small press magazines. A pamphlet *Cities like Jerusalem* is to be self-published soon and a book of short stories *Aegean Islands.*

Eugénie Murray Golding died in 2013 a few weeks short of her ninetieth birthday. In her long life she travelled widely, including a trip to China when it was unusual for Westerners to go there. She loved animals and it's sad she never realised her dream of visiting Borneo to see the orangutans which fascinated her. A founder member of VRWG, we remember her for her friendship, her forthright views – always tempered with great humour – her stylishness and, of course, her poetry.

Liz Sandbach is a freelance technical and scientific editor who relishes the opportunity to escape from left-brain thinking by writing creatively. She has been an active member of VRWG for the past nine years and also of the North West Poems and Pints scene. She divides her time between Cheshire and the Dordogne. Liz lives in hope that one day Colin Firth will come to his senses and realise his true destiny – but failing that, Dominic Cooper will do!

Marian Smith lives in Warrington with her husband and chickens. She currently spends far too much time in the office but her master plan is to finish her novel, sell the film rights to Steven Spielberg and retire to a remote Greek island.

Val Sullivan was a talented writer who will be well remembered for her gentle humour and generous spirit when encouraging her fellow writers. She was instrumental in getting our first anthology produced so it is a fitting tribute that she should be part of this one. Val died in June 2008 after a courageous battle against cancer. She left behind great memories, an unfinished novel and some wonderful poetry.

Bill Webster is 60 years of age chronologically, albeit not mentally or intellectually, and lives in Cheshire with his wife Helen and an annoying Jack Russell terrier called Ross who seems determined to outlive him. He enjoys surfing and shooting, but not at the same time. (Bill, not the dog.)

Liz Wells lives in Cheshire. Apart from the day job, she spends most days being the servant to a very mischief-loving Westie pooch. Liz's favourite types of writing are prose and poetry. She also has a love of photography (the camera goes everywhere), textile crafting and being outdoors. Liz shares her love of writing on her Facebook page **www.facebook.com/loveofwriting**

Printed in Great Britain
by Amazon.co.uk, Ltd.,
Marston Gate.